7th Heaven™

NOBODY'S PERFECT

BY AMANDA CHRISTIE

Based on the hit TV series
created by Brenda Hampton.

Based on teleplays and stories by
Brenda Hampton and Charles Lazer.

Random House   New York

Library of Congress Catalog Card Number: 99-64539
ISBN: 0-375-80433-1

Printed in the United States
August 1999
10 9 8 7 6 5 4

ONE

Outside the Camden home, the bright spring sun warmed the grass, which was still damp with morning dew. Sunlight danced through the tiny bathroom window. Matt could even hear birds singing in the trees.

Funny, he thought with a smile, *I've never noticed the birds before. I wonder if they sing like that every morning?*

Humming along with the sparrows, Matt checked his reflection in the mirror. *Not quite right,* he decided.

Giving his long, wavy light brown hair another pass with the brush, Matt realized that today was different. Special. His hair finally in place, he gazed into the mirror, considering his reflection again.

He was wearing his best suit and favorite tie. His clothes were neatly pressed. His shoes were shined.

Matt wanted more than anything to make the right impression. He placed the brush on the counter and adjusted his tie.

Okay, he thought. Now he was ready to go...except for that strand of hair that stubbornly continued to fall over his forehead.

With an impatient sigh, Matt lifted the brush and started over.

Downstairs, the Sunday morning bustle in the Camden house had ground to a complete halt. The family—with one exception—was gathered in the kitchen. Mrs. Camden was clearing the breakfast table. Lucy and Mary were helping, too.

"Has anybody seen Matt?" Mrs. Camden asked as she placed the vase of flowers in the exact center of the kitchen table.

Lucy and Mary, both dressed in their Sunday best, traded meaningful looks.

"He was in the bathroom," Lucy replied after a pause.

"Probably a major hair prep," Mary added.

Rev. Camden looked up from his morning sermon, which he was still fine-tuning. "A major hair prep for church?" he asked incredulously.

"I don't think so, Dad," Mary replied knowingly. "Sounds a little more serious than church to me."

Clutching a worn pencil, Rev. Camden shook his head and turned his attention to the work. Suddenly, he squinted and looked up.

"Honey," he called to his wife, "I was just looking at this quote from Robert Frost—I thought I used another poem here."

Mrs. Camden turned to face her husband. She wore a conservatively tailored gray suit that accentuated her eyes.

"No," she replied, gathering the last few glasses from the table. "Actually, you had a hole there with a little bit of Frost's 'The Road Not Taken'—misquoted, I might add."

She smiled at her husband. "Everybody uses that poem, honey," she continued. "So I put in a better one."

Rev. Camden nodded and turned back to his sermon.

"Mom?" Lucy asked, picking up the butter dish. "Have we got anything planned for this afternoon?"

Mrs. Camden looked at her daughter and shook her head. "No. Why?"

"Oh, nothing," Lucy replied. "It's just that there's an opening on the cheerleading squad, and I thought I might give it a shot…if I can get some practice in."

Mary rolled her eyes in disgust.

"I didn't know you were interested in cheerleading," Mrs. Camden said.

"Yeah, why not?" Lucy said, nodding. "One of the girls dropped off the squad, and they're holding open tryouts this week."

Her parents and Mary all exchanged looks.

Mrs. Camden cleared her throat. "Well, that's great," she said.

Lucy understood the expressions on all of their faces. "What?" she demanded defensively. "I know I'm not ready *today*. But with a little practice I *could* learn how to do it. Cheerleading is not exactly like brain surgery, you know!"

I'll say, Mary thought, staring in disbelief at her younger sister.

As Lucy huffily carried the butter to the

refrigerator, she stumbled over her platform shoes. Rev. Camden, Mrs. Camden, and Mary exchanged another look.

Just then, Matt burst into the kitchen. He slammed right into Simon, who was standing in the doorway, arms crossed. Simon's face was a mask of concentration. Matt halted abruptly as his little brother tumbled to the kitchen floor.

"Are you okay, Simon?" Matt said, reaching down to help him up. "I'm sorry, man. I didn't see you!"

As Simon rose from the floor, he smiled brightly at his older brother's words. "That's okay," Simon said, his smile broadening. "I'm fine. In fact, I'm *great!*"

"Great?" Rev. Camden said. "And why is that, Simon?"

The blond-haired boy turned and faced his father. "Thanks to Ninja mind control, I am entering the first stages of invisibility."

"And why would you want to be invisible, son?" Rev. Camden asked.

Simon shrugged his shoulders. "Invisibility has its uses, Dad," he answered mysteriously.

Filled with a burst of newfound confidence in his magical powers, Simon rushed out of the kitchen. Happy, the dog, followed at his heels, barking.

Little Ruthie, who had been staring at her brother the whole time, turned to her parents with a puzzled look.

"Can *you* see him?" she asked. Rev. Camden and Mrs. Camden both nodded. Ruthie, shaking her head in obvious bewilderment, followed Simon out of the room.

"Hey, Dad," Matt asked, "can I have the car keys?"

"Why?" Rev. Camden replied. "Can't you just ride with the rest of us?"

"I've...I've kind of got a date," he replied sheepishly.

"You're not coming to church because you've got a *date?*" Rev. Camden replied, frowning.

"No, Dad," Matt reassured him quickly. "I'm bringing her to church."

"Oh," Mary cried. "*This* should be fun."

"So all of you have to be on your best behavior," Matt added, looking right at Mary. She shot him an innocent smile, as if to say, "Who, *me?*"

"We'll try," Mrs. Camden said diplomatically.

With a resigned sigh, Rev. Camden handed his oldest son the car keys. Matt felt everybody staring at him.

"What?" he said.

"Oh, nothing," Rev. Camden said. "What's her name?"

"Tia!" Mary and Lucy said in unison.

Matt faced his sisters. "You wouldn't know that if you weren't listening in on my phone calls," he said.

Mary and Lucy both shrugged and Matt headed for the door. Then he stopped and turned back to his father.

"Oh, and Dad?" he added. "Could you say something really, you know, profound or something? I kind of built you up so she'd want to come today."

Rev. Camden smiled at his son. "If you wanted 'profound' in my sermon, you should have told me weeks ago."

As Matt disappeared out the back door, Rev. Camden turned to the rest of his family.

"Has Matt ever brought a date to church before?" he asked.

"Nope!" Mary and Lucy replied, again in unison.

Mrs. Camden playfully touched her husband on the arm.

"I hope you can take the pressure, honey," she said with a smile.

TWO

The tall white doors on the large red-brick church opened wide. Rev. and Mrs. Camden came out, followed by the entire congregation. Rev. Camden wore his robe and held a Bible in one hand. He stood at the entrance and greeted his parishioners. As the members of the congregation shook his hand, Lucy raced to the family's station wagon.

"At *last*," Lucy cried, rolling her eyes. "I never thought Dad would shut up today!"

"Hey, wait up, Lucy!" Mary cried, catching up to her younger sister. "What's your hurry, anyway?"

"I've got to get home," Lucy declared. "I have to start practicing."

Mary grabbed her sister's arm.

"Practicing for *what?*" she demanded. "That silly cheerleading thing? You should forget about that."

Lucy stared at her sister. "Why?" she demanded.

"Because it's *stupid,* that's why," Mary declared, crossing her arms.

"Oh, right!" Lucy shot back. "Cheerleading is stupid, but throwing a big orange ball into a net is a service to mankind?"

"At least basketball is a *sport,*" Mary insisted. "Cheerleading is just making a spectacle of yourself. Cheerleaders don't actually *do* anything. They just cheer as the boys do everything."

"So that's how it is!" Lucy declared. There was anger and hurt in her eyes. She pulled away from her sister and rushed toward the family station wagon.

At the door of the church, at the very end of the congregation, Matt came out with a lovely teenager on his arm. She had short brown hair and dark, intense eyes.

"Dad, this is Tia Jackson," Matt announced. Then he turned to the girl. "Tia, this is my dad," he said proudly.

Tia shook hands with Rev. Camden. "Nice to meet you, Reverend," she said.

"Nice to have you with us," Rev. Camden added. "I hope you weren't bored."

Tia quickly shook her head. "Oh, no!" she insisted. "I absolutely loved your sermon. It was so...so deep."

Rev. Camden nodded, a trace of pride on his handsome face. Matt nodded proudly, too.

"I told you she was terrific," he stated.

"And perceptive, too," Rev. Camden added.

Tia smiled at them both. "I think it's so neat to see someone's parents at work," she gushed. "Work is so much a part of what people are—whether it's working in the home, like Mrs. Camden, or in the community. You know what I mean?"

Rev. and Mrs. Camden both nodded in agreement.

"Both kinds of work are such important contributions to society," Tia said to Mrs. Camden.

"Thank you," Mrs. Camden said, nudging her husband. "I don't hear that often enough nowadays."

Then she turned to her son. "Matt, if you two don't have any plans, why don't you bring Tia over for Sunday dinner later?"

Matt looked down at his feet, then toward his date. "Well, actually, I was thinking we'd just grab something on our own," he said.

But Tia touched his arm, interrupting him.

"Actually," Tia said, "if it's no trouble, Sunday dinner with the family sounds really nice."

Matt shrugged his broad shoulders. "Uh, sure," he mumbled. "I guess that would be okay."

"But only if you let me help, Mrs. Camden," Tia insisted.

"Great!" Mrs. Camden said with a bright smile. "Matt, could you pick up some ice cream on your way home?"

"No problem," he replied.

Then Matt put his arm around Tia and led her down the church steps to the car. At that moment, Simon and Ruthie burst out of the church.

Simon looked at his father accusingly. "Gee, Dad," he cried. "Do you have any idea how long the line for the bathroom is when you go into overtime?"

Rev. Camden shrugged and shook his head.

"You should give us a two-minute warning or something," Simon continued.

"Yeah," Ruthie, still fidgeting, chimed in. "Like they do in football."

Then Simon spotted Matt and Tia heading for the family station wagon. He raced down the steps to join them, shouting, "Matt! Tia! Wait up!"

Back at the church door, Rev. Camden nudged his wife. "Nice work," he whispered conspiratorially. Mrs. Camden gave her husband a puzzled look.

"What are you talking about?" she asked, pulling Ruthie into her arms.

"Inviting Tia to dinner, I mean," Rev. Camden added.

"And why is that?" she replied.

He gave a wise smile before answering.

"No one gets through dinner at the Camden house without revealing *something* interesting…"

"No!" Matt said, his arms outstretched as if to ward off his little brother. "No way are you coming with us. I mean it. Go home with Mom and Dad."

Simon kept on coming as Matt opened the door for Tia.

"Please," Simon pleaded. "You won't even know I'm here."

"Yeah," Matt replied. "And that's exactly my point. If I don't know you're here, then you might as well ride home with *them*."

Realizing he was getting nowhere with his brother, Simon turned to Tia. "Please," he begged, "can't I just ride with you?" His innocent eyes were wide.

Tia smiled, her heart melting. "Come on, Matt," she argued. "You can bring your brother along. It'll be fine."

Matt, knowing all was lost, threw up his arms in mock surrender. "Oh, all right," he cried, opening the back door. "Get in!" he said, shoving his little brother into the back seat.

Simon grinned triumphantly as he slid into the back. As Tia settled in the passenger seat, Matt got behind the wheel.

"Hey, Tia," Simon said. "Do you believe people can become invisible?"

Tia glanced at Matt, who chuckled. Then she turned and looked at Simon in the back seat. With all the seriousness she could muster, Tia replied, "Absolutely."

Simon leaned forward until he was hanging over the seat between them.

"I'm learning to direct my psychic energy and other people's perceptions so that they can't see me," he announced excitedly.

"Wow!" Tia replied, acting impressed.

"Okay," Matt declared. "Can you direct our perceptions so we can't hear you, either?"

Simon laughed. But Tia, who didn't want to see Simon mocked, came to his defense.

"I think it is entirely possible for someone to be invisible, Simon," she declared, a flicker of sadness crossing her pretty face.

"Do you really think so?" Simon asked enthusiastically.

"Yes, I do," Tia said almost in a whisper. "But you should be careful. Sometimes being invisible can be a bad thing…"

A deep sadness took hold of Tia's pretty face. Sensing a change in the mood, Matt jumped in. He peered into the rearview mirror, catching his brother's eye.

"All right, kid," Matt commanded. "Disappear."

Flashing a bright smile, Simon gave

Matt the thumbs-up. Then, as promised, he sank down into his seat until he disappeared from view.

Tia laughed in delight, then turned to Matt. "Can we stop by my house so I can change?" she asked.

"Whatever you wish, my dear," Matt replied graciously as he drove away from the church.

An hour later, the family was back home. Rev. Camden was helping his wife in the kitchen while Mary and Lucy played in the backyard. Matt, Simon, and Tia had not yet arrived with the dessert.

The kitchen counter was crowded with food and fresh loaves of bread. A shallow glass pan was awaiting the roast beef. As Mrs. Camden dragged the roast out of the refrigerator, she also snatched a plastic bag full of fresh green beans from the vegetable bin.

"Green beans? Let me help you with that!" Rev. Camden volunteered.

"Be my guest," Mrs. Camden replied, walking to the counter to prepare the meat for roasting. Rev. Camden pulled open a drawer and withdrew a plastic utensil.

"What are you doing?" she asked.

He held up the cooking utensil proudly. "I thought I'd slice them, you know?"

As he spoke, he thrust a single bean through the slicer, which cut it into four neat pieces.

"Voilà!" Rev. Camden announced, holding up the green bean with a dramatic flourish. "I give you French-cut green beans."

Mrs. Camden shrugged, unimpressed. "Okay," she sighed. "If that's what you want."

Rev. Camden continued to cut up the beans as his wife prepared the roast. Observing a particularly well-cut bean, he turned to her. "Do you know that when I was a teenager, I thought French-cut green beans were somehow connected to French kissing?"

Mrs. Camden shook her head. "When you were a teenager, you thought *everything* was connected to kissing."

Taking her reply for an invitation, Rev. Camden leaned into her face for a quick kiss. To his surprise and disappointment, she ducked under him and returned to her cooking.

Puzzled, he stared at his wife. "What?" he asked.

"What?" she replied innocently as she sprinkled salt and pepper on the meat.

He caught his wife's eye. "Did I do something wrong?" he asked.

She turned away, looking down at her work. "No," she replied coolly. "But it wouldn't hurt if you tried a more romantic approach. Once in a while, at least."

He smiled, trying to draw her out. "What could be more romantic than French-cut green beans, in our very own kitchen with our very own French bean slicer?" he asked, cutting up another bean.

Mrs. Camden looked at him again. "I don't know," she answered briskly. "You tell me."

He threw up his hands. "I'm lost," he declared.

"Oh, never mind, honey," she said. "It's not you...it's me. I was just watching Matt and Tia in church today, and I was thinking about us..."

"Us?" Rev. Camden said, still perplexed.

"You know," Mrs. Camden continued. "What we were like when our relationship was new. Before the family and the responsibility of your ministry."

She met her husband's puzzled expression.

"Those days were always so full of wonderful surprises."

"Oh, yeah," he said, a faraway look in his eyes. "I remember…"

For a moment, both of them fell silent, lost in their memories of a simpler time.

"Well?" Mrs. Camden said after a moment, breaking the silence. Rev. Camden, looking startled, turned to his wife.

"Well what?" he asked. For a moment, she stared hard at him. Then she threw up her hands.

"Oh, nothing," she announced finally. "I guess I'm just being silly."

Then she leaned against her husband. "Our life is still full of the wonderful," she said. "There are just not as many surprises anymore…And I miss them."

She gave her husband a quick peck on the cheek. Then she lifted the pan with the roast in it and headed for the oven. Rev. Camden watched her cross the kitchen, wondering what he should do next.

Mary, wearing beat-up jeans, practice sneakers, and a flannel shirt, measured her shot carefully. She balanced the basketball on the tips of her fingers, aimed, and shot.

The ball swished through the hoop.

Retrieving the basketball, Mary drib-
bled it a few times. Then, before taking
another shot, she stole a glance at her little
sister.

Lucy was on the grass, stretching her
hands and flexing her muscles. Then she
took a few quick steps, dropped into a dive,
and tried for the tenth time to do a cartwheel.

Once again, Lucy ended up facedown
in the grass.

Undaunted by her failure, she hopped
back up to her feet and dusted the grass
and dirt off her sweatpants. Then she
skipped over to her older sister.

"Mary," she asked, "can you spot me
while I do some more cartwheels?"

"*More* cartwheels?" Mary replied skeptically. "I haven't seen you do *any* cartwheels yet!"

"I'm working on it," Lucy argued. "So
can you spot me?"

"No," Mary said, dribbling.

"Why not?" Lucy cried. "When *you*
wanted to go out for basketball, I helped
you practice, didn't I?"

Mary bounced the ball, then tucked it against her hip. "That was different," she announced.

Lucy tossed her long hair over her shoulder. "What's different now?" she asked, genuinely confused. "You're my sister. You wanted something, and I helped you get it."

"Look," Mary said, lifting the ball and taking another successful shot. "If you want to be a cheerleader, I can't stop you. But I don't have to participate in your complete downfall as a woman and human being."

Lucy blinked. "Excuse me?" she said, bewildered.

Mary threw another shot. As it swished through the hoop, she spoke. "Don't you get it?" Mary demanded harshly. "Cheerleading totally trivializes women and women's sports."

Lucy sighed. "Thanks for your support," she said evenly.

Still steamed, Mary retrieved her ball. Lucy stood in the grass, staring at her older sister in disbelief.

"All I'm asking for is a little help," Lucy said, almost pleading.

"If you were going out for basketball,

or even gymnastics, then I'd be glad to help you," Mary declared, aiming the ball. "But cheerleading? Forget it."

Mary turned away from Lucy, still shaking her head. She launched the basketball through the hoop for the fourth time. As it came bouncing back to her, Tia appeared at the back gate.

"Hi," she said brightly. "Matt said you'd both be out here."

"Here we are," Mary said.

"Hi," Lucy said, still looking surprised and a little upset by her older sister's stinging words.

"Are you both shooting hoops?" Tia asked.

"No," Mary replied, staring daggers at Lucy. "Some of us don't *play* sports."

Tia, oblivious to the hostility simmering between the sisters, said, "You guys are so lucky. I'm an only child, and I always thought it would be fun having a brother or sister to hang out with."

"Not always," Lucy replied, staring right back at her older sister.

Mary bounced the basketball once, then tucked it under her arm again. "I'm going inside," she declared.

Thinking she'd somehow gotten in the

way, Tia moved forward to stop Mary. "No," she said. "Wait a minute. I'll go. You stay. Do whatever you were doing together."

"That's okay," Mary replied politely. "I've seen enough bad cartwheels for one day."

Shooting a parting glance at Lucy, Mary went inside. Tia and Lucy stood together, watching her go. When the back door slammed, Tia turned to Lucy.

"I'm sorry," she apologized. "Seems like all I have to do is show up somewhere and a war breaks out."

"No," Lucy said quickly. "Forget it. This has nothing to do with you, Tia."

A cloud passed over the older girl's face. "I've heard *that* one before," she muttered, almost to herself.

"Heard what?" Lucy asked innocently, missing Tia's sad expression.

"Nothing," Tia replied with a wave of her hand. "So," she continued, "you were doing cartwheels?"

"Yeah!" Lucy said enthusiastically. "Wanna see one?"

Tia nodded. Lucy crossed the grass. She flexed, took a deep breath, and began to run. But when she went up onto her hands, she lost her balance and landed hard on the ground again. She immediately jumped to her feet, spitting out grass.

Tia winced. *Ouch,* she thought sympathetically. But she kept a smile plastered across her face.

"Why don't you try it again?" Tia suggested helpfully.

In the kitchen, Happy stared curiously at Simon. The boy stood still, leaning against the counter. His eyes were closed and his face was scrunched up in deep concentration. His arms were folded over his chest and his breathing was deep and even.

The dog, utterly confused, tilted her head and whined in curiosity. But Simon refused to budge or acknowledge Happy's presence.

Mrs. Camden opened the refrigerator door and pulled out a carton of milk. Then she crossed the room, passing by Simon as if he weren't there. Mrs. Camden approached Ruthie. The little girl sat on a high stool, pouring almonds into a measuring cup.

Some of the nuts spilled out of the cup and onto the counter.

"That's enough, sweetie," Mrs. Camden

declared. "Just half a cup."

Nodding, Ruthie set down the box of almonds and lifted the measuring cup. More almonds spilled out.

"Now pour the almonds into the green beans," Mrs. Camden instructed. Ruthie poured the nuts into a casserole filled with the French-cut green beans. Then she looked up at her mother.

"Good!" Mrs. Camden declared. "Now mix the nuts and the green beans together with your hands."

Ruthie nodded and dived right in. Beans and nuts spilled everywhere, but Ruthie was careful. She picked them up from the countertop and put them back into the pan.

At that moment, Matt came in. He, too, walked past Simon as if he weren't there.

"Have you seen Tia?" Matt asked.

"No, honey," Mrs. Camden answered, shaking her head.

"Have *you* seen Tia?" Ruthie asked Matt innocently, still stirring the beans.

Matt glanced at his little sister. "No, I haven't, Ruthie," he replied. "That's why I'm looking for her."

"Well," Ruthie said, "if nobody's seen her, then maybe she's invisible."

Simon came out of his mystic trance for a moment. He turned and snickered at Ruthie. Matt blinked before replying.

"Tia is anything but invisible," he noted.

Mrs. Camden caught her son's eye. "Tia seems very nice," she said. "How many times have you gone out with her?"

"Counting last night? Twice," Matt answered with a lovestruck look. "But it was like…well, like this instant connection between us, you know?"

Mrs. Camden nodded, recalling a time long past. "Yeah, I know," she said. "It was that way with me and your dad when we first met." Matt noticed that his mother had a faraway stare. He gave her a curious look.

Suddenly snapping back to reality, Mrs. Camden quickly added, "Of course, your father and I were much older than you and Tia! Much, much older."

Matt, knowing he'd pushed one of his mom's buttons, continued on.

"Oh, of course, of course," he stated with a mischievous twinkle in his eyes. "But you have to admit that kids *do* grow up a lot faster these days," he added slyly.

As Matt headed for the back door, Mrs.

Camden shook a warning finger at her son. "Some do, and some don't," she said.

Matt nodded. "I'm going to find Tia."

When Matt went out the back door, Mrs. Camden lifted a stack of dishes. As she headed for the dining room, she turned and spoke to her "invisible" son.

"Simon," she said. "Would you put out the napkins, please?"

Stunned, Simon opened his eyes. Then he noticed Happy sitting in front of him, still staring at him curiously.

"You know, Happy," Simon suggested, "if you'd stop following me around, people wouldn't be able to see me."

"Oh, yes, we would," Ruthie said confidently. Then she grabbed the casserole dish full of green beans and followed her mother to the dining room.

THREE

The pleasant Sunday dinner was nearly over.

The main course had been cleared away, and half-empty dishes of chocolate ice cream sat before everyone still sitting at the table. Simon and Ruthie, who had already finished with their dessert, had gone off to get ready for bed.

Tomorrow was a school day, after all.

The Camdens sat across from Matt and Tia. Mary and Lucy watched their older brother's new girlfriend with mounting curiosity. Matt beamed proudly.

Finally, Tia finished her dessert. She set down her spoon and looked up at her hosts.

"Thank you for dinner, Mrs. Camden,"

Tia said. "Can I help you clear the rest of the dishes?"

"Oh, no," Mrs. Camden replied with a wave of her hand. "If Mary and Lucy are both finished, they can do that."

The two sisters rolled their eyes, but refused to glance at each other. Lucy was still mad that Mary hadn't helped her learn cartwheels. Mary was still angry that her little sister wanted to be a cheerleader.

Mary and Lucy both rose and began clearing the table. A few minutes later, they were done. The girls excused themselves and went to their room, still not speaking to each other. Their parents noticed the tension between them.

"I really feel guilty for not helping out," Tia said. "That was part of our agreement," she reminded them. "That I'd come to Sunday dinner if you would let me help."

"I think you should relax, Tia," Rev. Camden said.

"So what are your plans for the future?" Mrs. Camden probed. "Do you want to go to college?"

Tia nodded. "I'd like to major in economics," she replied. "I think it's a valuable thing to study if you plan to become a homemaker."

"Is that what you plan to do?" Mrs. Camden asked. "Become a homemaker?"

Tia nodded. "I think family is very important," she declared. "Maybe the most important thing in the world. And *raising* a family is probably the most important *job* in the world."

"Well, thank you again for saying that, Tia. Sometimes I can feel a little taken for granted, *just* being a mom and all," Mrs. Camden said.

"Oh, no," Tia argued. "You should never feel that way, Mrs. Camden. Matt tells me you're a great mom."

"Wow," Mrs. Camden said. "We're certainly enjoying *your* company."

"I agree," Rev. Camden said as he smiled and put down his spoon. "It's not often that anyone in this house wants to talk about my sermons after church," he added, punching Matt playfully on the shoulder.

"I thought your sermon this morning was just wonderful," Tia declared. "And I thought the Robert Frost poem you quoted was so beautiful, and perfect for the occasion."

"Yes," Mrs. Camden said, looking at her husband. "It *was* a good choice, wasn't it?"

"I'm surprised you're familiar with 'The Death of the Hired Man,'" Rev. Camden said, avoiding his wife's gaze.

Tia nodded. "Oh, yes," she said. "It's in our English lit book, but I never heard it read out loud before. I thought it was the perfect way to end your sermon. The safe choice would have been something like 'The Road Not Taken,' but that wouldn't have been nearly as effective."

"No, it wouldn't have been. Especially if it had been misquoted." Mrs. Camden nodded to her husband.

Rev. Camden frowned, ducking his wife's stare.

"You know," Mrs. Camden continued, "when we first started dating, Rev. Camden wrote some wonderful poetry himself."

"Wow!" Matt exclaimed. "What did the Colonel think about that?"

Rev. Camden looked at his son. "Your grandfather, the Colonel, is a fairly poetic guy for a Marine Corps veteran," he said.

Matt laughed. "I'll bet your poems aren't anything you could read in church, huh, Dad?"

"Oh, I wouldn't say that," Rev. Camden replied.

"*I* would," Mrs. Camden said. "His poetry was very personal."

Tia smiled, then met Rev. Camden's gaze. "Could you quote the Frost poem again?" she asked.

Rev. Camden, almost blushing, replied. "Oh, I don't know. I think we've had enough eloquence for one day."

"That's right," Matt interjected. "We don't want to have to call the poetry police."

Tia, still looking at Rev. Camden, spoke again. "Please," she pleaded. "Just a line or two..."

Rev. Camden glanced down at his empty dish, hesitant to do a repeat performance.

"Go on, honey," said his wife. "I thought you were pretty terrific myself."

"Please," Tia added. "Do the line about home."

As Tia and Mrs. Camden watched, Rev. Camden switched into poetry mode. He scrambled to recall all the lines, finally settling on the one he was sure he remembered correctly.

After he had finished, Tia held Rev. Camden's look. She appeared to be very affected by what he had said. Then tears welled up in the young woman's eyes. She shot up from her chair, mumbling an apology.

"Excuse me," she said as she ran from the table, sobbing.

Mrs. Camden, as surprised as the rest of the family, reached across the dinner table and touched her son's arm.

"Matt, honey," she said. "You need to go see about her."

"Me?" Matt declared, caught totally off guard. "But Dad was the one who made her cry!"

"Your mom picked the poem!" Rev. Camden cried defensively. Mrs. Camden looked at her husband, then at her son. Matt withered under her gaze.

"Okay, okay!" Matt said, surrendering. "She just threw me off for a second, that's all."

As Matt rose and left the table, Rev. Camden looked at his wife. "What do you think that was all about?" he asked.

Mrs. Camden shook her head. "I don't know," she replied. "But Tia is obviously in a lot of pain."

Pushing his chair back from the table, Rev. Camden began to rise. "Should I...?"

"No," Mrs. Camden said immediately, pushing him back into the chair. "Give them some time first."

After looking in the kitchen and the library, Matt found Tia in the darkened living room. She was leaning against the fireplace mantel with her face buried in her hands.

Matt heard her choke back a sob as he entered the room.

"Tia?" he whispered. "Are you...are you okay?"

Tia looked up, wiping tears away from her dark eyes.

"Come on," Matt insisted, approaching her. "Tell me what's going on."

Tia took a deep breath, trying to regain her composure. Finally, she smiled weakly.

"Sorry," she apologized, attempting to sound as if everything was all right. "I generally try not to burst into tears unless I'm alone in my room."

Matt put his arms on her shoulders and pulled her close to him.

"Hey, that's okay," he said. "We're big on emotions around here. It's a Camden thing."

Then Matt leaned down and kissed Tia

on her cheek. She wiped away another tear and smiled up at him.

"I guess this is going to sound pretty silly…" she began.

"No," Matt insisted. "Nothing that makes you cry would sound silly to me. I just want to know what's wrong, that's all."

Tia sighed. "I guess it doesn't sound like such a big deal nowadays," she confessed. "But my parents…they just got divorced. I didn't want to tell you right away, your dad being a minister and all…"

"It's okay," Matt said, relieved it wasn't something much worse. "I'm really sorry about that."

Tia looked into Matt's eyes, a frown creasing her forehead. "You have no idea how lucky you are to be in this family," she said sincerely.

Matt touched her chin. "Yes, I *do* know," he replied. "And I also know how lucky I am to have met *you*, Tia."

Tears filled Tia's eyes once again as she leaned against Matt. He held her protectively, wanting nothing more than to comfort and protect her.

FOUR

Simon was having a pretty good day, even though it was Monday. His regular teacher hadn't shown up for geography class. Instead, they had been assigned a substitute. That gave Simon and his friends a chance to goof off a little bit. But then the substitute teacher, Mrs. Seidel, decided to quiz them by asking some tough geography questions. Simon began to panic.

Geography wasn't Simon's best subject, and he hadn't studied all weekend. Knowing that he would look pretty stupid if the teacher called on him, Simon saw only one way out. He crossed his arms and took deep, regular breaths. Then he used his Ninja mind powers to will himself invisible.

To his surprise, it worked. Mrs. Seidel didn't call on him *once* the whole afternoon. She called on everybody *but* Simon. She even called on Harry Holmes and Tony Fenzel three times each. And, each time, they didn't know the answer to her question.

Finally, near the end of the period, Mrs. Seidel began to talk about Japan.

Now *that* was a subject Simon knew something about. After all, Japan was the home of the Ninjas, whose secrets of mind control he'd been practicing all weekend long.

"What is the capital city of Japan?" Mrs. Seidel asked the class. A few hands shot up immediately, but she ignored them. Instead, she pointed to Harry again.

"Mr. Holmes," she asked, "do *you* know the capital city of Japan?"

Harry frowned, clearly stumped. "Ah… Brazil?" he said uncertainly.

The whole class exploded in laughter. Simon uncrossed his arms and laughed with the rest of them.

"Mr. Camden," Mrs. Seidel said, hushing up the class, "do *you* know the answer?"

Simon, realizing he'd let down his

guard and was now visible to his teacher, swallowed hard.

"Tokyo," he said finally. "The capital city of Japan is Tokyo!"

"Excellent," Mrs. Seidel declared. "And I can see that you haven't even covered that material yet. You must be a very smart young man, Simon."

Simon smiled proudly.

"Mr. Holmes could take a lesson from you, Simon," the substitute added.

Simon, still basking in the triumph, looked at Harry Holmes.

Uh-oh, he thought when he saw the look on Harry's face.

Harry and Tony were both glaring at Simon, who immediately turned away. When Simon stole another glance at the pair, Harry was shaking his fist at him.

Just then, the bell rang. Quickly, the students filed out of the room. Harry and Tony were the first to leave. Simon had a bad feeling that they were waiting for him.

Just like that, what had started out as a good day had suddenly taken a turn for the worse. For the rest of the afternoon, Simon watched over his shoulder for Harry and Tony. They were two guys you just didn't want to cross.

Finally, near the end of the afternoon, Simon was cautiously heading for the playground when he saw the two bullies. They were sitting on the steps by the door to the playground.

Simon knew they were waiting for him.

Suddenly, over the heads of a bunch of other kids, Harry spotted him. Simon immediately turned around and headed in the opposite direction. Tony and Harry followed, pushing through the crowd of kids.

Simon rounded the corner of the hallway, wondering what he should do next.

Wait a minute, he reminded himself. *I have the power to twist perception and make myself completely invisible.*

Slowly, Simon backed toward the wall near the door to geography class. When his back was pressed against the cool plaster, he closed his eyes, folded his arms, and willed himself invisible.

They cannot see me if I cannot be seen, he said to himself. *They cannot see me if I cannot be seen...*

Just then, Harry and Tony came around the corner. But at that same moment, Mrs. Seidel opened her classroom door. Simon was now behind the open door, totally hidden from view.

Simon's eyes were still closed, the magic words still running through his head. He had no idea that the classroom door was covering him.

"Where's Camden?" Harry asked his friend.

"Beats me!" Tony replied, looking around. "I thought he went this way…"

"Maybe he snuck out to the playground," Harry suggested. "Let's go look there."

Behind the door, Simon could hear Harry's and Tony's every word. He dared not open his eyes, fearing that the Ninja mind spell might be broken if he did.

As the two boys departed, Mrs. Seidel closed the door. So when Simon opened his eyes, he was standing in plain sight. But the two bullies were gone. All Simon saw was an empty hallway.

"All right, it worked!" he cried, pumping his fist in triumph. "I *am* invisible!"

Meanwhile, at the nearby high school, Tia caught Matt on the stairwell between classes.

"Hey, *there* you are!" Tia cried.

Matt put his arm around her. "Are you okay?" he asked.

"Yeah," she said, nodding quickly. "I'm just fine. But I need to ask you a big favor."

"Anything," Matt replied. "Just name it."

"I hate to ask, but I really need a ride to my dad's place after school."

"Sure," Matt said. "No problem."

"It's my week to stay with him," Tia explained. "He was supposed to pick me up last night, but he was busy." She shook her head sadly. "He didn't even call, probably because he was afraid he'd have to talk to my mom..."

"Sounds pretty rough," Matt said sympathetically. Tia nodded but said nothing.

"Well, I'll take you over right after I drop off the kids," Matt continued.

Matt was about to take off for his next class, but Tia caught his arm.

"Maybe you could hang out at my dad's with me," she suggested hopefully. Matt tilted his head in curiosity.

"Oh, *he* won't be there," Tia said with a frown. "He'll be on some date tonight, I'm sure," she added wistfully. "He's *always* got a date."

Matt stared down at his feet. The offer was tempting. Finally, he spoke.

"Tia, I'd *like* to hang out with you

tonight. Believe me, I'd like nothing more. But I've got homework...a paper that's due at the end of the week." Matt shrugged. He felt bad that Tia might be disappointed, but he knew he wouldn't have time to finish his paper if he went to Tia's dad's house.

Tia quickly sensed rejection in Matt's reply. Her eyes dropped and her frown deepened.

"Oh, sure," she said. "I understand."

Seeing her disappointment, Matt added, "Or we *could* do our homework together."

Tia's dark eyes lit up, and she smiled brightly. "I've got an idea!" she said.

Matt nodded quickly as the halls emptied around him. He was worried he'd be late for his next class.

"You take me to my dad's so I can drop off my stuff, and then I'll follow you back in my car."

"You have your own car?" Matt said in amazement. Tia nodded.

"My dad bought it for me," she told him. "But I can't take it to my mom's 'cause he doesn't want her to drive it."

"I, ah, I see," Matt replied. The hallway was completely empty now. And he still had to get to the other end of the building.

"So I'll follow you to your place—then you won't have to take me back later or anything," Tia suggested. "I can just drive myself."

"Sure, great," Matt said. "Pick you up later." He held out his hand, and Tia slipped into the curve of his arm. She smiled up at him.

"Do you think your mom will mind if I stay for dinner again?" she asked. Matt shook his head.

"No. No way," he replied. "I'm sure it'll be fine." As they walked off arm in arm, the late bell rang.

He was late for class, but he didn't even care.

To Mrs. Camden's surprise, the kitchen door swung open and her husband walked in. As she finished making her peanut butter and jam sandwich, she smiled at the unexpected surprise.

"Late lunch?" Rev. Camden asked. Mrs. Camden nodded as she cut the sandwich into two neat triangles.

"I've been so busy today that I haven't had time to stop and eat anything," she said.

Rev. Camden sniffed the air. "Ah, peanut butter and grape jelly—"

"It's jam, actually," Mrs. Camden interjected.

"Ah, peanut butter and grape *jam*," Rev. Camden corrected himself. "What a delicious aroma."

"To what do I owe this unexpected visit?" Mrs. Camden asked, wiping her hands on a towel.

"My meeting ended early," Rev. Camden replied, sidling up to her. "I thought I'd come home and get some work done here." He searched the room. "Where's Ruthie?"

"Play date," Mrs. Camden replied, pouring herself a glass of milk.

"Wow!" Rev. Camden exclaimed. "You mean we're all alone?"

"That's right," Mrs. Camden nodded.

"All alone in this big, empty house in the middle of the afternoon," Rev. Camden hinted.

"Mmm-hmm," Mrs. Camden nodded again, lifting the sandwich to her mouth.

"With at least an hour to kill before the kids get home from school?" Rev. Camden continued.

"You got it," Mrs. Camden answered,

preparing to enjoy her sandwich.

Rev. Camden shook his head and smiled. "That's why I like spontaneity," he said. "Sometimes it pays off." With a hopeful look in his eye, Rev. Camden tried to hug his wife. But she had other ideas and slipped away from his grasp.

"I don't think so," she said, her hand warding him off.

"Hey, wait a minute," Rev. Camden insisted. "Weren't you the one who said you missed the surprises in our relationship?"

"Mmm-hmm," Mrs. Camden answered, her mouth full of peanut butter and jam.

Rev. Camden threw his arms wide. "Well, surprise!" he announced. "Here I am!" He made another grab for his wife, but she dodged him again.

"Oh, no, you don't, buster!" she cried. "You call coming home early a *surprise?*"

"You *are* surprised, aren't you?"

"No, Eric. Don't you get it?"

He shook his head, and Mrs. Camden rolled her eyes.

"A surprise would be if you actually planned something," she cried. "Something romantic, something that took a little effort on *your* part!"

The reverend dropped his arms with

disappointment on his face. "So my spontaneity means nothing to you?"

"Of course it does," Mrs. Camden countered, handing him a sandwich triangle. "It means you can have half of my peanut butter and jam sandwich."

Mrs. Camden walked into the living room. The reverend looked down at the sandwich in his hand. Then he dropped it onto the plate. Brushing crumbs off his hands, he turned and headed for the back door.

"Maybe I'll go back to the office and finish up a few things," he announced.

"Don't forget to pick up Mary after basketball practice," Mrs. Camden called from the living room. "I want you to have that little talk with her, just like you promised."

Rev. Camden nodded as he went out the door.

Outside Walter Reed Junior High School, Lucy Camden spotted two of her friends. But instead of calling to them, she ran up behind the pair, who were totally engrossed in their conversation.

As she got closer, Lucy heard part of their discussion. To her horror, she discovered they were talking about *her*.

"Lucy Camden making the cheerleading squad would be scarier than *The X-Files!*" Peggy Zimmer snickered.

The statement froze Lucy in her tracks. Suddenly, she turned to flee. But something stopped her, and she continued to listen to their conversation.

"Can you believe it?" Nancy Kiley added. "Lucy is the biggest klutz in the school."

"I know," Peggy added. "Those cheerleading pyramids will be even more dangerous with Lucy on the squad!"

"So, are you going to tell her?" Nancy asked.

"No way!" Peggy replied. "She's my friend."

"I know how you feel," Nancy said. "I couldn't do it either."

"Maybe we should ask Jimmy Moon to warn her," Peggy suggested. "It's for Lucy's own good, after all."

The two girls giggled uproariously. Finally, they walked on, never noticing that Lucy was standing right behind them.

When they were gone, Lucy raced toward the parking lot, where her brother was waiting for her. She found Matt sitting on the hood of the family station wagon.

"Get in the car!" Lucy demanded. Her face was bright red with embarrassment. She pulled open the door and jumped inside.

"Come on!" Lucy insisted. But Matt just stood looking at her through the open window.

"Hey, Sis," he asked calmly. "What's up?"

"Nothing," Lucy replied. "Just get in the car."

Matt nodded. "Okay," he said. "Just as soon as you tell me what's wrong."

Lucy met her brother's curious stare. "I'm a dope," she replied finally. "That's what's the matter."

"Oh," Matt said, smiling. "And why is that?"

"I'm a dope to think I could ever go out for cheerleading," she said, "and actually make the squad."

"Of course you can," Matt insisted.

Lucy just glared at him. "Oh, you think so?" she asked. Matt nodded. "Then you're a dope, too!"

"Come on," Matt insisted. "Tell me what happened."

"Nothing happened," Lucy said, cutting him off.

Matt leaned into the window, right into his sister's face. "Fine," he said. "It doesn't matter. I'm going to help you get on the cheerleading team anyway."

"*Squad,*" Lucy insisted, rolling her eyes. "It's a cheerleading *squad*. It's not a team."

"Team, squad, whatever," Matt said. "I'm helping you get on it."

"Yeah, right," Lucy said skeptically. "Like you know anything at all about cheerleading." She sighed, remembering her friends' cruel words.

"You may know something about basketball, Matt," she continued. "But you don't know a thing about cheerleading."

At that moment, several older girls from the junior high school cheerleading squad passed the Camdens' car. They were wearing their uniforms and talking among themselves. Lucy, totally humiliated, sank down in her seat until they passed.

But the cheerleaders didn't notice her anyway. They were all checking out Matt instead.

He smiled at them, causing them to burst into hysterical giggles.

"As a matter of fact," Matt replied, still smiling, "cheerleading is a topic I've studied quite closely for many, many years."

Matt leaned into the car window again. "Clear your calendar for the rest of the week," he announced. "Starting tomorrow, you're putting yourself in my capable hands."

"What are you going to do?" Lucy asked. Her brother's confidence made her curious.

"I'm going to turn you into a cheer-leader," Matt replied.

"But what are you going to do, *specifically?*" Lucy said.

Matt winked at her and shook his head. "Just trust me," he replied, giving her a thumbs-up.

As Matt crossed to the other side of the car, Simon popped up from the back seat. Lucy was startled and jumped up. Then she gave her little brother an angry look.

"You little turkey," she cried, outraged. "You were eavesdropping!"

"No, I wasn't," Simon said. "I was invisible."

As Matt climbed in behind the wheel, Lucy turned to her older brother.

"Did you know he was back there?" she demanded.

Matt looked at Lucy sheepishly. "I forgot," he admitted.

"You forgot because I'm invisible," Simon stated confidently.

"Oh, yeah?" Lucy replied. "Then how come I can *see* you, you little twerp?"

Simon smiled wisely. "When a person is suffering from violent emotions, it is very difficult to control their perceptions."

Lucy groaned and hid her face in her hands. Matt started the car, put it in gear, and drove away.

FIVE

Mrs. Camden rolled the vacuum cleaner into the closet just as the doorbell rang.

When she opened the door, a strange sight greeted her. Tia, holding an overnight bag, smiled at her. A light jacket was draped over her arm. Beside Tia was a woman wearing the distinctive red blazer of a well-known real estate company. The woman ignored Mrs. Camden and continued to talk into her cellular phone.

"Hello, Tia," Mrs. Camden said, staring at the older woman.

"Hi, Mrs. Camden," Tia replied. "This is my mom." Tia looked at her mother, who was still talking into the phone. Tia nudged her.

"Mom," she said. "This is Mrs. Camden."

"Sorry," the woman said, covering the phone with her hand. "I got this call just as we got out of the car." She sighed. "You know how it is," she said before returning to her conversation.

"No, Mom," Tia said, rolling her eyes. "She *doesn't* know how it is." Then Tia turned to Mrs. Camden, her face red with embarrassment. "I'm sorry," she said.

"It's okay," Mrs. Camden replied sympathetically. "Really."

"Well, I'll tell them," Tia's mother said loudly into the phone. "But I really don't think that they'll go for it."

Tia and Mrs. Camden exchanged glances. As her mother continued with her conversation, Tia spoke to Mrs. Camden. "I hope it's all right," she said. "Matt agreed to take me to my dad's house."

"Oh, sure," Mrs. Camden replied with a wave of her hand. "Matt will be home any minute."

"He was going to pick me up," Tia added, still trying to cover her embarrassment. "But Mom wanted to drop me off here instead."

Tia's mother snapped the cellular phone shut with a loud click.

"Hi, I'm Ellen," the woman announced, sticking out her hand for Mrs. Camden to shake. "I would have taken Tia to visit her father myself, but frankly, we haven't exactly been on friendly terms since the divorce."

"Oh, I'm sorry," Mrs. Camden replied. "That must be very hard," she turned and looked at Tia. "On both of you."

Mrs. Jackson shook her head. "Actually," she said with a sigh, "I'm perfectly content having no contact with him whatsoever. I'd much rather have Matt take her over there. It was very nice of him to offer."

"He should be here soon," Mrs. Camden informed them. "Would you both like to come in...perhaps have something to drink? I just made tea."

"Oh, thanks," Mrs. Jackson replied. "But I can't. I've got a couple coming over to look at our house. Some other time, perhaps."

"You're selling?" Mrs. Camden asked.

Mrs. Jackson nodded. "It's a tough market," she stated. "And Tia knows I mean no offense by this, but a home looks much better without a teenager running around."

"Of course," Mrs. Camden said, somewhat baffled by Tia's mother.

"We're moving to a singles complex," Mrs. Jackson announced. "It's a smaller space, but at least I'll have a better shot at...well, *you* know."

Leaning toward Mrs. Camden, Tia spoke. "She means she'll have a better chance at meeting someone," she said.

"Hey," Mrs. Jackson said. "If he can do it, then I can do it, too." Then the real estate agent looked around the foyer of the Camdens' home.

"This is a nice place you have here. A very nice place," she noted. "With a little work, you could get a nice price for this house. There's lots of space, and the design is so traditional."

Mrs. Jackson turned and faced Mrs. Camden. "If you don't mind my asking, just how much did you pay for this house?"

Mrs. Camden, appalled at such a rude question, tried to cover her reaction. "We don't...*own* the home," she replied. "It belongs to the church. My husband is a minister."

Mrs. Jackson flashed Mrs. Camden a knowing look and a smile.

"I told you that, Mom," Tia said. "Don't you remember?"

"Did you, dear?" Mrs. Jackson replied. Then she turned to Mrs. Camden again. "I hear that men of the cloth are so hot! Is that true?"

Before Mrs. Camden could reply, Mrs. Jackson continued on. "If he has any single friends, keep me in mind, would you?"

As Mrs. Camden struggled to keep her jaw off the floor, Mrs. Jackson gave her daughter a quick kiss. Then she was out the door.

"Gotta run," Mrs. Jackson called over her shoulder as she rushed to her car. "Call me if you need anything, sweetie!"

As Mrs. Jackson drove off, Mrs. Camden put her arm around Tia.

"She's really not a bad person," Tia explained. "She just likes to stay busy. Her work keeps her from thinking about the divorce."

Mrs. Camden sighed. "Divorce is hard on everyone in the family," she said to the girl.

Tia looked into Mrs. Camden's eyes. "Believe me," she said, "the marriage wasn't a picnic, either."

Seeing the sadness in Tia's expression, Mrs. Camden smiled encouragingly and gave the young woman a warm hug.

Rev. Camden looked up past the steering wheel of his car and saw Mary come out of basketball practice. She seemed very animated. She high-fived a couple of her friends and then chatted with a few of her teammates.

"Mary!" Rev. Camden called. "Over here."

Mary waved to her dad as he got out of his car and began to walk toward her. Then she said her good-byes and met her father in the middle of the parking lot.

"What a great practice!" Mary exclaimed when she reached him. "I had four steals. I wish I could play that well *every* day."

"That's terrific," Rev. Camden declared, patting his oldest daughter on the back.

"It was incredible, Dad," she continued. "I couldn't do anything wrong today. I was in the *zone!*"

"Have I told you lately how proud I am of you?" Rev. Camden said.

"Sure, Dad," Mary said, smiling. "But I still like to hear it. Everyone likes to be appreciated."

Rev. Camden nodded. It was the same thing his wife had been telling him, although in not so many words.

"Well, it takes a lot of discipline to be good at a sport," Rev. Camden said. "Any sport—or any athletic endeavor at all," he added.

Mary halted in her tracks and looked at her father. She sensed a lecture coming.

"What's up, Dad?" Mary demanded.

"Look, hon," Rev. Camden began. "I know you think it's stupid, but cheerleading takes talent, determination, and plenty of hard work, too."

Mary rolled her eyes. "I just wish I could get Lucy interested in a *sport,*" she said sadly. "Something *besides* cheerleading."

"But it's what Lucy wants to do," Rev. Camden insisted.

"But, Dad, do you know *why* there's a sudden opening on the cheerleading squad?"

Rev. Camden shook his head. "No," he replied.

"Because a girl fell off the top of the pyramid and broke her collarbone!" Mary replied.

"Ouch!" Rev. Camden winced. "What pyramid?"

"You know," Mary insisted. "They pile themselves on top of each other until there's one poor girl at the top—way up in the air."

"Why?" Rev. Camden asked, totally confused.

"I don't know! You tell me!" Mary cried. "Why would anyone take that kind of a chance...and for *what?* What's the point, anyway?"

Her father shrugged. "I suppose some people feel that way about athletics, Mary. You could get hurt pretty badly playing basketball, you know."

"Yeah," Mary agreed. "But at least it wouldn't be from something klutzy and embarrassing, like slipping on a pom-pom and falling twenty feet to the floor."

"Still," Rev. Camden argued, "it *is* Lucy's choice."

Mary faced her father. "That's why *you* have to talk her out of it, Dad," she said. "Before something really disastrous happens."

Rev. Camden blinked. "Like what?"

"Like she makes the squad," Mary replied.

"People do some pretty stupid things growing up," Rev. Camden stated. "I seem to remember something about a tattoo…"

Mary threw up her arms. "I was a lot younger then."

"Mary," Rev. Camden replied, "that was six months ago."

"Like I said, I was a lot younger then," she said with a smile.

Rev. Camden took his daughter's arm and walked with her for a while. Finally, he turned and faced her.

"Your sister is your biggest fan, Mary. She comes to every one of your games—"

"And?" Mary interrupted.

"And she really looks up to you," he continued. "I know cheerleading doesn't mean that much to you, but isn't it enough that it's important to Lucy?"

"Dad," Mary said evenly, "it's *cheerleading*."

Rev. Camden threw up his arms, surrendering. "Yeah, I know," he said. "But I promised your mom I'd give you a lecture."

Mary smiled up at her dad. "Well, that one was…pretty good," she said.

"Thanks," Rev. Camden replied, laying an arm over her shoulder. "But do me a favor," he added.

"Sure, Dad," said Mary.

"Some of that stuff I just said *was* pretty good," he said. "So think about it...okay?"

"Okay, Dad, I will," Mary promised. "But I still think cheerleading is stupid."

Simon was feeling good. He was thinking of all the ways he could use his newfound powers. When his mom told him it was time for bed, he didn't even argue. He went upstairs and put on his pajamas. Then he went into the bathroom to brush his teeth. When he was finished, he decided to try out his powers of invisibility one more time.

He pushed open his bedroom door, and Happy rose from the bed to greet him. Her tail was wagging happily. But to her disappointment, Simon stopped her.

"No, Happy," he said. "Stay away from me, and I think this will work."

Simon scanned the room. *Good*, he thought. *I'm all alone*. Then he stood perfectly still.

Taking a deep breath, Simon closed his

eyes. Then, folding his arms over his chest, he began to recite his words of power. "They cannot see me if I cannot be seen," he whispered. "They cannot see me if I cannot be seen—"

But suddenly his concentration was broken when he heard Ruthie's voice.

"Hi, Simon."

"Ruthie?" Simon said. "Is that you?"

"Yes, Simon," she replied.

Simon looked around the bedroom. There was no sign of his sister anywhere.

"Where are you?" Simon demanded.

"I'm invisible," Ruthie giggled.

"Come on, Ruthie," Simon said, creeping toward the closet. "Come out. You're not fooling me."

Simon ripped the closet doors open. But to his surprise, Ruthie wasn't there. He looked around the room again, but still could find no sign of his little sister.

Then Simon remembered the time she hid under the bed. He tiptoed toward the bunk beds. "Come out, come out, wherever you are!"

Ruthie giggled. "I *am* out," she insisted. "I'm just invisible."

Quickly, Simon dropped to the floor and peered under the bed. There was nothing there but a few of Ruthie's old dolls.

"You can't be invisible, Ruthie," Simon argued. "You don't know how to be invisible."

"Can you see me?" the mysterious voice asked.

"No," Simon confessed.

"Then I guess I *do* know how to be invisible," Ruthie's voice said.

In desperation, Simon turned to Happy.

"Go, girl," he commanded. "Go find Ruthie…find her, girl!"

Happy's ears perked up, and she wagged her tail and barked. But she didn't move. Simon glared at his dog.

"Fine, then!" he cried, throwing up his arms. "I give up." Angrily, Simon marched to the door and, with one last look, he left the room. He slammed the door behind him, revealing Ruthie.

She had been hiding behind the door the whole time.

Happy barked again when she saw the girl. Ruthie giggled in triumph.

Matt sat on the living room couch with his textbooks stacked all around him. One book was open on his lap. He was scribbling facts from a graph onto his messy study sheet.

Lying on the couch with her feet on his lap, Tia tossed a pillow into the air. She had finished her homework and was obviously bored. Unfortunately for her, Matt had that big paper due at the end of the week. He couldn't quit now, as much as he would have liked to.

As he worked, Tia wiggled her toes. Matt smiled. Then he reached out and tweaked her foot with his pencil.

Tia giggled. So Matt did it again.

This time, Tia hit him with the pillow she was tossing in the air.

Just before a full-blown pillow fight erupted, the sliding double doors opened.

Rev. and Mrs. Camden were standing in the doorway.

"Sorry to bother you," Rev. Camden said. "But we just wanted to tell you that it's late, so we're going up to bed now."

"Good night," Mrs. Camden said.

Tia smiled at Matt's parents. "Good night," she said cheerfully. "And thank you so much for the dinner. I really enjoyed it and the conversation."

"I'm glad," Mrs. Camden said with a smile.

Tia looked at Rev. Camden. "I'm really sorry we didn't get to talk more. Maybe tomorrow?"

Rev. Camden looked at his son, who shook his head in understanding. Then he turned to Tia.

"Sure," he said. "I'm sure we'll get a chance to talk tomorrow."

"So," Tia said, "I guess I'll see you then."

Rev. Camden nodded. "Good night," he repeated.

"Yes," Mrs. Camden chimed in. "Good night again."

Rev. Camden gave one last look to Matt. Then the couple slid the living room doors closed and went upstairs to bed.

Tia sighed contentedly and settled deeper into the soft couch. Matt looked at her, then cleared his throat.

Finally, he turned and faced Tia. She smiled up at him.

"I, ah, I hate to tell you this," Matt began. "But them coming in like that was really Camden code for 'It's late, and you should send your guest home.'"

"Oh, okay," Tia said, blushing. She immediately sat up and began to put her shoes on.

"It's so great having dinner together, hanging out, just doing stuff that normal families do..."

"Well," Matt said, gathering her books together into a neat pile, "I don't know how normal we are, but I'm glad you had a good time."

Matt placed Tia's books on the coffee table. Then he stood up and stretched his stiff muscles. He glanced at his watch and was surprised to see how late it was. He turned to Tia, still sitting on the couch. She seemed unwilling to leave.

Matt stretched out his hand and Tia took it. He pulled her up from the couch. To his surprise, she leaned into him and gave him a kiss. When their lips parted, Tia turned her head and looked into Matt's eyes.

"Are you sure you don't want me to stay just a little longer?" she asked.

Matt felt tempted, but it didn't seem right after his parents' visit.

"I *do* want you to stay," he sighed sadly. "But it's a school night and I still have some reading to finish. Besides, I don't want to go against my parents' wishes."

Tia nodded, then stood on her toes and kissed him again. "Thanks again for taking me to my dad's this afternoon," she said. A cloud passed over her face. "Someday maybe he'll actually be home and I'll introduce you," she added.

Matt instantly sensed Tia's sadness. He struggled with his own feelings—he knew he should stay home, but he also felt he should help her in any way possible.

"I could follow you in my own car," he announced. "That is, if you don't really want to drive home alone."

Tia smiled and gently touched his nose with her finger.

"No, silly," she said. "The whole point of picking up my car was so you wouldn't have to do that."

Matt was unconvinced.

"I'll be fine. I drive myself home all the time," Tia continued.

Matt smiled as he took her arm. "Then let me escort you to your carriage, my princess."

"Oh, do, Prince Charming," Tia replied with a laugh and wave of her hand.

Together, they sauntered out to her car.

Upstairs, Rev. and Mrs. Camden lay awake with the problems of the day occupying their thoughts.

"Did you have that talk with Mary?" Mrs. Camden asked her husband.

"Talk?" he said defensively. "I thought you wanted me to lecture her."

"Honey," she informed him, "your talks *always* sound like lectures. It's the minister in you."

"Oh, thanks," the reverend replied.

"Well?" Mrs. Camden prodded.

Rev. Camden nodded. "I talked to her about Lucy wanting to be a cheerleader," he said. "She listened, but I don't know how much actually sank in. You know how stubborn Mary can be."

"Mmm-hmm," Mrs. Camden nodded. "She's a lot like her father."

Rev. Camden shook his head. He dreaded where the conversation could go, so he quickly changed the subject.

"I can't believe that story you told me about Tia's mother," he said.

Mrs. Camden sat up in bed. "You should have been there," she said. "Or maybe it was better you weren't—she might have made a play for you."

"Was it really that bad?" Rev. Camden asked.

"Worse," his wife replied. "She said that 'men of the cloth are so hot.' Those were her *exact* words."

"Was Tia embarrassed?" Rev. Camden probed.

Mrs. Camden nodded. "She tried to cover it up, but I was embarrassed for her."

"Divorce is so hard—the way it hurts everyone," Rev. Camden reflected.

"Yes," Mrs. Camden replied. "You know, I think Ellen doesn't even realize that her daughter is suffering."

Rev. Camden shook his head, finding it hard to believe. "Well, hopefully, Tia has a better relationship with her father," he replied.

"He bought her a car," Mrs. Camden added. "That has to count for something."

Rev. Camden nodded, but he wasn't sure he agreed with his wife. Material things were easy to come by—all you needed was the money. But love and caring for your family was more rare—and much more precious.

Rev. Camden stifled a yawn and checked the grandfather clock in the corner. He kissed his wife good night and turned the light off.

"I wonder how Ellen Jackson knows so much about ministers?" Mrs. Camden wondered aloud in the darkness.

* * *

Tia saw the Camdens' bedroom light go off.

Sitting behind the wheel of her car, she reached for the keys, still in the ignition. But when she tried to start the car, her hands began to shake. Tears welled up in her eyes.

A feeling of emptiness opened up inside her, filling her up completely. She feared it would swallow her whole.

She looked longingly at the Camden house. Tia wanted nothing more than to go to the door, ring the bell, and cry on the reverend's or Mrs. Camden's shoulder.

But she knew she couldn't. That would be too embarrassing. And risky—Tia feared she would lose the relationship she had with the Camden family if she asked for too much from them.

Sighing, she reached for her keys again. But tears began to blind her. She buried her face in her hands and began to sob uncontrollably.

The phone buzzed beside Rev. Camden's ear. He opened his eyes instantly. He answered after the second ring, hoping that the noise hadn't awakened his wife. But as she had fallen asleep cradled in his arms, his sudden movement woke her up. She looked at her husband as he put the phone to his ear.

"Hello?"

"Yeah, hi," said a smooth male voice. "Listen, I'm sorry to wake you up, but my name is Bob Jackson—I'm Tia's father…"

The reverend immediately sat upright in his bed. "Yes, hello. I—"

But Mr. Jackson's voice, and another sound, interrupted him. It seemed as if Mr. Jackson was whispering something to another person. The reverend could hear a young woman giggling on the other end of the line.

Then Mr. Jackson came back on the line. "Tia's not back yet. I was hoping I might find her over there. I'm a little worried about her," he added, almost as an afterthought.

Rev. Camden looked at the clock. It was two-thirty.

"Mr. Jackson," he said anxiously, "I thought she left hours ago. Let me go downstairs and check. I'll call you right back."

He hung up and then turned to face his worried wife.

"It seems that Tia didn't make it home."

SIX

Rev. Camden threw on his robe and rushed out of the bedroom. Mrs. Camden was right behind him until she saw where her husband was headed.

Rev. Camden flung open Matt's bedroom door. To his surprise and relief, Matt was sleeping soundly. He didn't even notice the intrusion.

As Rev. Camden quietly shut the door, he turned and faced his wife. He smiled reassuringly.

They headed downstairs. Rev. Camden checked the couch, but it was empty.

"Hey," Mrs. Camden said. "I think I found her."

In the driveway, in the front seat of a sporty black car, Tia was sleeping sitting up. The Camdens approached the car and saw a wad of tissue still clutched in her hand.

The car's interior lights went on once Mrs. Camden opened the door, and Tia woke up. She rubbed the sleep out of her swollen eyes and tried to smile.

"Are you okay?" Rev. Camden asked softly.

Tia nodded. "I'm fine," she said. "I just didn't feel like going back to my dad's tonight."

The reverend helped the girl to her feet. "Your dad just called. He was very worried about you," he said.

Tia sighed and checked her watch. Then she rolled her eyes. "So worried that it took him until two-thirty to notice I'm not there?"

The Camdens heard the sadness in the girl's voice.

"Come on, let's let him know you're okay," said Mrs. Camden.

Tia nodded. She began to shiver in the cool evening air. Mrs. Camden draped her robe over Tia's shoulders. Together, they went into the house.

When they got to the living room, Rev.

Camden called Mr. Jackson, who answered after the first ring.

"Hello, Bob," he began. "It's Eric Camden. Tia's fine. She's right here."

"Oh, good," said the voice on the other end of the line. "I had a feeling she was." The reverend could hear relief in Mr. Jackson's voice. He also heard the woman in the background once again.

"I could drive her over there," Rev. Camden suggested. "Or we could put her up here for the rest of the night."

When Tia heard that, she smiled. Mrs. Camden smiled back, but cautiously. She was beginning to see Tia's situation more clearly.

"I don't want to put you out," Mr. Jackson said.

Rev. Camden looked up at his wife. She nodded uneasily. "No trouble at all," he said. "She'll be fine. Would you like to talk to her?" he added.

"No," Mr. Jackson replied. "That's fine. I'm sure she's in good hands."

"Well, good night, then," Rev. Camden said uncertainly. But Mr. Jackson had already hung up.

"Let me guess," Tia said, still smiling.

"It's okay with him if I stay here."

Rev. Camden nodded.

"Sorry if I scared you," apologized Tia. "I was going to drive home in the morning, before anyone woke up."

She turned and looked at Mrs. Camden. "His dates are always gone by then," she said.

Mrs. Camden put her arm around Tia's shoulder. "Don't worry about it," she soothed. "We'll make up a bed on the couch."

Tia gave Mrs. Camden a big hug. Over the girl's shoulder, Mrs. Camden shot her husband a meaningful look. The reverend nodded sadly, rubbing his eyes.

How could a father treat his daughter like that? he wondered.

"Thanks," Tia whispered. "To both of you."

"Tia, does your father know how you feel about his dating?" asked Rev. Camden.

"I don't think it makes a difference how I feel," she replied with a shrug.

He wouldn't take that as an answer. "It *might*, you know," he replied softly. "Maybe you should have a talk with him."

Tia hung her head for a moment. Then she looked up and smiled.

"You really *do* believe in miracles, don't you?" she replied.

"You kind of have to in my line of work," Rev. Camden replied.

He looked at her. She met his gaze with one of her own.

At least she's still fighting, he thought. *Her spirit isn't broken...yet.*

The reverend, Mrs. Camden, and Tia were just finishing breakfast the next morning when they heard Happy bark. The dog dashed into the kitchen, followed quickly by Simon. Matt brought up the rear, but stopped dead in his tracks when he saw his girlfriend. He noticed that she was still wearing the same clothes as last night, which meant she had never gone home.

"Tia!" Simon cried out in delight.

"Hey, Simon," Tia said, throwing her arms wide and giving the boy a hug.

Matt walked up to the table. "Are you okay?" he asked anxiously. "Did you have car trouble or something?"

Tia smiled at him. "It's a long story," she said evasively.

"She'll tell you all about it later," Mrs. Camden said. Then she looked at her younger son. "Simon," she announced, "it's time for breakfast."

"In a minute, Mom," Simon pleaded. "After I talk to Tia."

Simon grabbed Tia's arm and led her to the other side of the kitchen.

"I think I figured out why Happy follows me around, even when I'm invisible," Simon whispered in a serious tone.

"Really!" Tia said. "Why?"

"Well," Simon began. "According to the Ninjas, when I'm invisible, I don't really disappear—"

Tia raised her eyebrows in polite surprise. "No?"

"No," Simon continued. "I'm still there. All I did was use my mental powers so that you can't *see* me."

"Of course," Tia agreed instantly.

"But a dog has greater mental powers and can sense I'm still around."

"So Happy can still sense your presence," Tia said, nodding in mock understanding. "Good point."

"Yeah," Simon said. "Until school yesterday, I really thought I couldn't do it. Then I figured out that Happy was the problem."

"Well," Tia said, patting him on the back, "keep up the good work."

At that moment, Ruthie ran into the kitchen, followed by Mary and Lucy. Mary's eyes widened when she saw Tia.

"Was there a sleepover?" Ruthie asked innocently.

Mary leaned close to Lucy. "Doesn't she ever go home?" she whispered to her sister. Lucy held back a giggle.

"Morning," Tia said to the girls. Then she turned to Mrs. Camden. "Thanks for breakfast. Sorry to eat and run, but I should go home and change my clothes before school today."

"You don't have to go, Tia," Simon insisted. "You can wear something of Mary's."

Mary shot her brother a sour look, but he didn't see it.

"Did I hear something?" Mary asked Lucy. "A strange, stupid voice?"

"It's Simon," Ruthie insisted. "He's not invisible now."

"Too bad," Mary quipped. Then she looked at Matt's girlfriend. "Come on, Tia," she said. "Let's find you something to wear."

"Thanks," Tia said. "This is great. Almost like having real sisters."

Mrs. Camden looked over at her husband from the table. Rev. Camden already knew what she was thinking. He nodded, as if to say *Don't worry, it's under control.*

Mrs. Camden tilted her head and looked at her husband skeptically.

As Mary and Tia headed upstairs, Lucy followed behind. Simon raced to keep up with them.

"I'll go with you," he insisted. "I'll make sure she shows you the *good* stuff."

When the group disappeared up the steps, Matt sat down next to his father. He looked concerned.

"Look, Dad," Matt began. "I told her it was late and that she had to go home. I even said I'd follow her if she didn't want to drive by herself…"

"Your father and I found her asleep in her car," Mrs. Camden interrupted.

Matt shook his head in bafflement. "I don't get it."

"It's okay, Matt," Rev. Camden said. "We know you did nothing wrong."

Matt looked at his parents in relief. "Listen, Matt," continued the reverend. "Would it be okay with you if I paid her father a visit?"

Matt thought about it for a second. "Yeah, I guess," he finally answered. "But from what Tia says, he sounds like a jerk."

Rev. Camden nodded. "I kind of picked up on that," he remarked.

Matt turned to his mother. "What was Mrs. Jackson like?" he asked her.

Mrs. Camden frowned. "Pretty much like her dad," she replied. Matt clenched his fist and shifted in his chair. Then he looked at his father again.

"So," he said, "what are you going to say to him?"

Rev. Camden saw the concern on his son's face. "Listen, son," he reassured him, "I've done this kind of thing before. Many times."

"Yeah," Matt said cautiously. "But *this* time it affects me." His parents both looked at him.

"I mean, Tia likes our family, right?" Matt asked. His parents nodded.

"And we like her, right?" he continued. Again his parents nodded in agreement.

"Then look," Matt said. "I know it's still kind of early in the game, but I think that she could be the one."

Matt heard the girls laughing upstairs and stood up. "I'm going to go up and check on Tia," he said as he walked up the stairs.

His parents exchanged shocked glances. Could they have heard Matt correctly? Or had they misunderstood what he just said?

"Did he just say…?" Rev. Camden muttered. Mrs. Camden nodded with a faraway stare. "The *one*," she replied.

Rev. Camden shook his head. "Do you think she feels the same way about him?"

Mrs. Camden faced her husband. "I think Tia likes all of us Camdens—equally."

Oh, no, thought Rev. Camden. "Do you think we should tell Matt?"

"No," Mrs. Camden replied with a knowing shake of her head. "He'll figure it out soon enough."

"And if he doesn't?" he pressed.

"You know that one of the kids will tell him," said his wife. "Mary or Lucy, probably."

After a moment, Mrs. Camden took a look at her husband. "You're dressed up today," she observed. "Something special planned at work?"

"I think I'm going to pay a visit to Mr. Robert Jackson," he announced. "Tia's father. He's a big lawyer for a firm downtown."

Mrs. Camden nodded.

"I'll see you later, hon," he said, heading for the front door. But she cleared her throat before he could leave.

"Didn't you forget something?" she asked. Rev. Camden searched his pockets and pulled out his keys.

"What, these?" he asked.

Mrs. Camden looked annoyed. "A kiss!" she cried.

"Oh, right," mumbled Rev. Camden. Mrs. Camden looked up from her chair with her lips ready. Rev. Camden pecked her on the forehead and patted her shoulder.

"'Bye, honey," he called as he went out the door.

Mrs. Camden rose and put her hands on her hips, glaring at her departing husband. *How dare he ignore me when I pucker up*, she thought.

Out on the driveway, as Rev. Camden fumbled with his keys, he stole a look back at the house. He thought about his wife stewing, and it made him smile. *If Annie likes surprises, then she's going to love this one*, he thought, tingling with excitement. He couldn't wait for the look on her face when he finally sprang his trap.

*   *   *

That afternoon, Rev. Camden was ushered into the luxurious law office of Robert Jackson. The office, lined with oak, had large dark leather chairs that filled the corners. Two large chairs also occupied the area in front of an expansive, highly polished desk, also made of oak.

Mr. Jackson sat behind the desk, talking on the phone. He wore a dark, expensive suit with a silk tie. He was as tall as Rev. Camden, but a little older. His manner was as smooth as his voice was loud.

When his secretary showed Rev. Camden to a seat, Mr. Jackson covered the phone with his hand.

"I'll be with you in just a moment," he said. Then he went back to his telephone conversation.

"Is that a joke or an insult?" Mr. Jackson screamed into the phone. "Tell her she can settle now, or I'll advise my client to go for custody. Let's see how she likes *that!*"

Mr. Jackson slammed down the phone and dropped farther back into his leather chair. He looked at Rev. Camden.

"So?" he said. "Just what can I do for you?"

Rev. Camden rose and thrust his hand

across the desk. "I'm Eric," he said. "Eric Camden. Matt's dad? We spoke on the phone last night... or maybe I should say this morning."

"Oh, yes," Mr. Jackson recalled as he shook the reverend's hand. "Matt, right?"

The reverend nodded.

"Yes," Mr. Jackson continued. "The new boyfriend. It's good to see Tia getting out. It seems like she's doing a lot better now. For a long time, I thought the divorce was tough on her. All she did was sit around and sulk. But now—"

Just then, the phone buzzed again. Mr. Jackson lifted a finger and said, "Give me a second here."

Within seconds of picking up the phone, the lawyer exploded into another tirade.

"Maybe I didn't make myself clear!" he screamed into the phone. "This is not a negotiation. That was the offer, and it closes at the end of this business day. Do you understand?"

As the man spoke, Rev. Camden watched him in fascination. It was like watching a poisonous snake. It was ugly, squirmy, and dangerous—but you just couldn't look away.

Just then, the secretary entered and placed a lunch delivery on Mr. Jackson's desk. He winked at her and she giggled.

Instantly, Rev. Camden recognized that giggle. He had heard it over Mr. Jackson's phone last night.

"Look, it's up to you," Mr. Jackson continued. "But if you want me to tell you how to run your business, here's what *I* would do…"

Mr. Jackson smiled as he spoke. He reminded Rev. Camden of a shark he'd seen at the aquarium. The only difference was that *this* shark looked hungrier.

"I'd do what's best for your client," Mr. Jackson pressed. "Sell her on the thirty percent. It's still a lot of money, and she still gets the kids…and nobody has to hold a yard sale for her!"

Rev. Camden continued to watch with horrified fascination.

"Maybe I should talk to her," Mr. Jackson insisted. "*I* can sell her on this deal. What does she look like?"

Suddenly, his smile brightened, and he licked his lips.

"No kidding," he said into the phone. "She looks *that* good? Is she seeing anyone?"

At that moment, the secretary entered once again. "Your one o'clock appointment is waiting for you," she announced.

Still clutching the phone, Mr. Jackson looked at the reverend and shrugged. He covered the phone with his hand.

"I'm really sorry, Mr. Camden," he apologized. "It's just one of those days. Can we reschedule?"

The reverend rose. He leaned over the desk to shake the lawyer's hand again.

"I'll call you," Rev. Camden said, certain now that everything Tia said about her father was true.

Mr. Jackson flashed him a big grin, then returned to his telephone conversation.

SEVEN

Tia caught up to Matt in the school hall-way. He looked at her curiously, noticing something odd. Then he realized that she was wearing one of Mary's outfits.

"Hey, Matt," she greeted him, giving Matt a peck on the cheek.

"Hi, Tia," Matt replied, happy to see her.

"So," she said, fidgeting, "I was wondering if you could come over to my dad's house after school—or maybe we could go to your house."

Matt frowned. "Tia," he began, "I can't see you this afternoon. I promised Lucy I'd help her with something important."

Tia was disappointed, but tried not to show it.

"That's okay," she said sadly. "I think it's really nice that you spend time with your sisters. I guess I'll just hang out at my dad's tonight."

Matt touched her arm. "Hey, Tia," he said, "we'll have lots of time together this weekend. I promise."

Tia smiled brightly when she heard that. "Can we go to church again?" she asked. "I really liked hearing your dad speak from the pulpit."

Now it was Matt's turn to be disappointed. "Yeah, sure," he replied. "I guess so. But I was kind of hoping we'd get some time alone. Just you and me."

"Sure, that would be nice, too," Tia said halfheartedly. "But it's okay if we spend time with your family, too. I like them a lot. They're so nice to be with."

Matt smiled. "They feel the same way about you, too," he told her. Tia smiled again. Then she leaned against him and gave him a friendly kiss on the lips.

With that, she strolled away with a final wave of her hand.

After school, Lucy changed into practice clothes and met Matt in the parking lot. Matt refused to answer any questions about Tia, so they rode together in silence.

Finally, Matt pulled up in front of a large building. There was a sign above two sets of metal double doors that read GOLD MEDALIST GYMNASTIC TRAINING.

"You've got to be kidding," gasped Lucy. "What are we doing here?"

"I told you," Matt replied with a confident smile. "Leave everything to me."

"But—"

He held out one finger. "I said leave everything to me," he reassured her.

Matt walked Lucy to the entrance. When they entered the gym, a stunning young woman clad in leotards greeted them. She smiled warmly when she saw Matt.

"So this is your little sister," the woman said, looking at Lucy, who felt invisible next to such a glamorous young woman with such an athletic build.

"Hi, I'm Kristin," she said, offering Lucy her hand.

"Kristin, meet my sister, Lucy. She's going out for cheerleading."

"Hi," Lucy said shyly.

"We just need to work out a few things in the gym," said Matt.

"That's fine," Kristin said, handing

Matt a bunch of keys. "Just lock up when you leave and put the keys back through the mail slot."

"You bet," Matt replied, still smiling at the radiant woman. Kristin put a coat over her athletic gear.

"Thanks, Kristin, we really appreciate this."

"No problem," Kristin replied. Then she turned to Lucy. "Good luck."

Lucy just nodded.

Once Kristin had left, Lucy turned to her brother. "Who was *that?*" she demanded.

Matt blushed. "I, ah...I dated her sister."

Lucy met his eyes. "And?"

"And she dumped me," Matt said. "So Kristin figures she owes me. Now let's get started."

"Started with what?" Lucy groaned, daunted by all the equipment in the gym. Matt could tell she was nervous. He grabbed Lucy by the shoulders and turned her around.

"Face it, Lucy," he said sternly. "You know how to do everything it takes to be a cheerleader. You're just as good as anyone else trying out."

"Well…" Lucy sighed skeptically.

"You just need confidence, enthusiasm, and the determination to do it. That's the secret to doing anything you set your mind to."

Lucy considered her brother's words for a moment. Then she nodded nervously.

"Come on," Matt said, moving toward the parallel bars. "Let's get going."

Lucy had taken only two steps before she tripped on her shoelace and fell to the mat. She saw the loose shoelace and smiled at her brother weakly.

It's going to be a long afternoon, thought Matt.

But to his surprise, Matt was wrong.

At first, Lucy was clumsy. Her feet constantly slipped off the balance beam, and she wavered all over the place. But Matt was there to spot her the whole time. He watched her every move, made suggestions, and gave her what she needed most—encouragement. Soon Lucy was using her toes for balance and crossing the beam with the ease of a practiced gymnast.

As she continued to walk back and forth on the beam, Lucy realized that she didn't need Matt to steady her anymore. He saw it, too, and he stepped back to watch her form. *She actually looks pretty good for a first-time gymnast,* he thought.

When Lucy was comfortable with the balance beam, Matt moved her over to the horse.

He motioned to her to jump, but Lucy shook her head. She looked a little intimidated by the high piece of equipment.

"Come on and jump!" Matt said. But Lucy still shook her head.

"Okay, then," Matt said. "Watch me do it."

After watching her brother jump over the horse about ten times, Lucy felt she was ready to try. She took a deep breath, then got a running start.

To Lucy's shock and surprise, she vaulted right over the horse. Her form was sloppy, however, and she crashed into her brother. They both landed on the padded mats and then laughed hysterically.

"Let me try it again!" Lucy cried excitedly.

As the afternoon progressed, Lucy's confidence and abilities began to really improve. Sometimes she would forget Matt's advice or try something she wasn't ready for. But for each tiny step backward, she made two gigantic strides forward.

When they tried cartwheels, Matt told Lucy how to keep her balance.

"Don't bend your body so much. Just stay straight and dive into the turn."

Lucy tried another cartwheel, and then another. Once Matt thought she could do it on her own, he stepped back.

Lucy then performed a half-dozen perfect cartwheels in a row. Matt clapped and cheered her on the whole way.

She ran over to her brother and gave him a great big hug.

The next challenge was the uneven parallel bars.

The two bars stood on top of long metal poles. Lucy's heart raced as she faced them. Matt raised her over his head, and she clung unsteadily, her hands on the top bar.

"Get up there, Lucy," Matt said.

"I can't," Lucy cried nervously.

"Yes, you *can*, Lucy," Matt insisted. "I *know* you can."

Uncertainly, Lucy climbed up onto Matt's shoulders, supported only by the hanging bar. She wobbled unsteadily.

"Lock your knees," Matt said, struggling to hold her upright. "Lock your knees."

As Lucy locked her knees, her whole body became solid and straight. She could feel her own strength, and Matt could tell.

Lucy's heart began to swell with triumph. Bravely, she released her hold on the bars, supported only by Matt's strong shoulders. He lifted her even higher into the air, but instead of becoming afraid, Lucy threw her arms above her head.

She felt as if she were soaring, completely fearless and triumphant.

Matt clapped his hands together. Lucy jumped to the mat and landed smoothly, still erect and tall.

"You did it!" Matt cried.

Lucy raised her hands above her head in victory.

That evening, Lucy was hanging out with Mary in their room. While Lucy scribbled in her school notebook, Mary continued to admire the leather jacket she had found at a thrift shop after school.

"I can't believe I found this," Mary said. "And it was so cheap."

She turned to her little sister. "What do you think?"

"It's nice," Lucy replied noncommittally. "But a little retro."

"Of course it's retro. It's from the 1970s."

"Why would you want to wear something so *old*?"

Mary just rolled her eyes.

"So," she said casually a few minutes later. "I heard you and Matt practiced for the big tryout tomorrow."

Lucy nodded and went back to her homework.

Mary looked down at her sister. "So how did it go?"

Lucy just shrugged. "It went okay, I guess."

But from the look on her little sister's face, Mary knew she was hiding something.

She was just about to ask what when there was a knock on the bedroom door.

Mary pulled it open and found Tia standing there.

Tia handed Mary the outfit that she had borrowed, cleaned and pressed. "I wanted to thank you for lending me this," she said.

"No problem," Mary replied. "You didn't have to bring it back right away."

"I wanted to," Tia said, looking around the room.

"Hey, you want to see the jacket I found at the thrift shop?" Mary said. Tia nodded. Mary pulled it down and put it on.

"Wow!" Tia cried. "It looks really great on you."

"Thanks," Mary replied.

Then there was another knock. Mary opened the door, and Matt was standing there, looking at Tia with a big smile.

"Hey," Matt said. "Mom said you were up here. I thought you were at your dad's."

"I was," Tia replied. "I thought you were busy."

Matt looked at Lucy, who smiled. "That was before," Matt said. "But I'm free now. You want to do something?"

Tia turned and looked at Matt's sisters. As one, the three girls turned and looked at Matt.

"Nah," Tia said. "I'd rather hang out with the girls."

"Oh," Matt said, trying to hide his disappointment. He shrugged and closed the door. He could hear the girls giggling.

As Matt headed down the hall, he turned back to look at Mary's door. Simon walked out of his room and Matt bumped into him, which made Simon stop chanting his words of power.

"Simon!" Matt cried, annoyed. "Will you knock off this invisibility stuff. It's not funny anymore, and nobody else around here likes it, either!"

Simon shrugged. "You're just in a bad mood," he said. "I understand."

Matt lifted Simon off the floor. "Now, why would I be in a bad mood?" he asked.

"Come on, Matt," Simon replied. "You know."

"No, I don't," Matt said strongly, shaking his head. "Tell me."

Simon shook his head sympathetically. "I hate to be the one to break the news to you, but I think Tia wants to be a Camden."

Matt rolled his eyes. "Simon," he said. "I think it's a little too soon to think about marriage. Not that it couldn't happen down the line, of course..."

"Who's talking about marriage?" Simon said. "I think she wants Mom and Dad to adopt her."

"*What?*" Matt cried, shocked.

"Which would make Tia your sister," Simon realized. "Which would mean you can't go out with her anymore, much less marry her."

"Mom and Dad are *not* adopting Tia," Matt replied.

Simon shrugged. "Well, maybe not. But I still think she wants them to."

A shadow crossed Matt's face. "Why?" he asked, fearing the answer.

"Isn't it obvious?" Simon stated. "She needs a family."

Matt's eyes grew wide and his face looked startled. He leaned against the wall as if the wind had been knocked out of him. As Simon went back into his room, Matt considered his little brother's wise words carefully.

As Rev. and Mrs. Camden were preparing for bed, they discussed his very unsatisfactory meeting with Mr. Jackson.

"He seemed completely oblivious to the fact that Tia is having a problem," Rev. Camden said. "I just can't understand how he could be missing all of her signals."

Mrs. Camden shook her head. "Her mother was the same way. It's as if they can't see their own daughter. It's like Tia is invisible or something!" she said.

Then she noticed that her husband wasn't listening to her. He looked absorbed in concentration.

"Honey?" she said. "Are you okay?"

Rev. Camden shook his head, snapping

out of it. "Yeah, hon," he replied.

Then he stood up and began to pace back and forth. "I wonder what would happen if I got the two of them in the same room?"

"Ellen and Bob Jackson?" Mrs. Camden replied.

"Sure," Rev. Camden said. "If I get them together, maybe they can see what they're doing to their child."

Finally he stopped pacing and climbed into bed, looking at his wife. She was staring at him and shaking her head.

"What?" he said. "You don't think I should do it?"

"I think you can do anything you want," she replied, rather too sweetly. Then she gave him a kiss and turned out her light.

But Rev. Camden sat up and turned his light on.

Mrs. Camden gave him a surprised look. "What are you doing?" she asked.

"Oh, just thinking," Rev. Camden said. Mrs. Camden turned over and curled up on her side of the bed. The reverend smiled as if he had something up his sleeve. Then he turned out his light and went to sleep.

EIGHT

Morning came much too soon for Lucy Camden. She skipped breakfast because she was so nervous. As she got dressed for tryouts, she noticed her reflection in the mirror.

She was not happy with what she saw.

She suddenly flashed back to the group of cheerleaders who had passed by her the day she overheard her friends talking about what a klutz she was. Lucy remembered how confident, smart, and pretty they all were. She gazed at her reflection long and hard.

Lucy felt very, very ordinary.

A knock at the bathroom door interrupted her.

"Go away!" she yelled.

"Hurry up," Matt said from the other side of the door. "You'll be late."

Lucy opened the door and stepped out of the bathroom. Matt looked at her.

"Ready?" he asked.

Suddenly, her eyes filled with tears, and she tried to flee back into the bathroom. But Matt was faster. He grabbed her arm and pulled her out into the hall.

"Hey," he said, wiping a tear away with his thumb. "What's the matter?"

Lucy slumped against the wall, looking totally defeated. Then she met her brother's worried gaze.

"Look," she began. "I really appreciate what you did for me at the gym. But now...now I just don't know what I was thinking."

Lucy dropped her arms to her sides. "I don't stand a chance."

Matt grabbed Lucy's shoulders. "What are you talking about?" he demanded. "Everything you have to do at tryouts you did with me in the gym. I *saw* you do it, so we both know you *can*."

"Yeah," Lucy said, wiping her eyes. "I can do all the technical stuff. It's not that."

"Then what is it?" Matt demanded. "You have to tell me."

Lucy sighed. Then she said the words she dreaded to say out loud.

"I'm just not pretty enough to be a cheerleader. My legs are too skinny and my head is too big and—"

Matt wouldn't let her finish. He took her by the arm and pulled her into the bathroom. Shutting the door, he pushed Lucy in front of the mirror.

Still wiping tears away, Lucy gazed at her reflection again. She didn't see a difference from before. She still thought she wasn't pretty enough.

"I want you to look at yourself." Matt said. "Can't you see how beautiful you are?"

She shook her head.

"But you *are* beautiful!" Matt insisted. "As beautiful as any cheerleader I've ever seen. And you know I've seen a few," he added with a wink.

Lucy smiled for the first time that morning.

"Do you really think that?" Lucy asked. Matt nodded his head.

"I don't *think* it," he stated. "I *know* it."

Lucy looked at her reflection one more time. After looking long and hard, she smiled. Thanks to Matt's kind words, she felt pretty. She looked up at her brother.

"Even if I don't make cheerleader, it was all worth the effort just for this." She reached up and hugged her older brother. "Thanks, Matt."

"Don't worry, you'll make it, Lucy," he said confidently.

"And if I *don't?*" she asked.

"Then I've got the rest of the year to work with you," Matt said.

As he smiled at her, Lucy turned to the shower.

"Okay," she said in a loud voice. "You two can come out now."

To Matt's surprise, Simon and Ruthie peeked out from behind the shower curtain. Both had big grins plastered on their faces.

"We weren't listening," Ruthie pleaded. "We were just being invisible."

Happy suddenly jumped out of the shower, too. As Matt pushed them out of the door, he shook his head and turned to Lucy.

"Did you know they were in there the whole time?" he asked.

Lucy smiled and shrugged. "I forgot."

"You know," Simon said as they headed

down the stairs. "If anyone really believed I could be invisible, I could do it."

Lucy and Matt exchanged knowing glances. "That's the second time he's been right in two days," Matt said.

"What was the other time?" Lucy asked. Matt pushed his sister on ahead.

"Never mind," he said.

The cheerleading squad gathered on the Walter Reed Junior High School field. The girls were all wearing their black-and-white uniforms. On the field with them were a group of aspiring cheerleaders, who were wearing colorful practice clothes, not uniforms.

Among them was Lucy. She looked up from her stretches and saw Matt and the others watching her. She gave a tiny wave to her older brother. He gave her a thumbs-up in reply.

The Camdens sat together in the bleachers. Tia was there, too, sitting beside Matt. He gazed at her from time to time, but made no attempt to put his arm around her shoulder or sneak a kiss.

Not before we have a long talk, Matt decided.

As the squad leader put the girls through their paces, Lucy kept up with them. The air was filled with chants like "Go, Eagles, go!"

With each new cheer, move, or stunt, more of the girls were eliminated. The field began to empty, but Lucy held her own.

Even Lucy's toughest critic—her older sister—was impressed with her performance on the field. Mary watched Lucy's moves and became increasingly impressed. Finally, she couldn't help herself. She *had* to say something.

"Wow! I hate to admit it, but this is kinda cool!" she exclaimed.

Mrs. Camden, who'd seen Lucy trip over the same rug five times a week, couldn't believe what she was seeing. When Lucy perfectly executed a triple cartwheel, her jaw dropped.

Rev. Camden leaned toward his wife. "Am I just being a proud father here, or is she really good?"

"She's really good," Mrs. Camden replied.

As her family continued to watch in dis-belief, Lucy effortlessly leaped through a hoop made by two cheerleaders' arms. She landed gracefully, while the next girl who tried it landed facedown in the grass.

Mary turned to her older brother. "How did you do this?"

Matt smiled. "All I did was help her find some confidence."

"Cool," Simon added. "Maybe cheerleader Lucy was invisible because all we could see was just regular Lucy."

Rev. Camden put his hand on his youngest son's shoulder. "I think you're exactly right, Simon," he said, beaming with pride.

Finally, the competition was down to the big moment. As the Camdens watched anxiously, the cheerleading squad formed up for the pyramid. Adding to the excitement of everyone in the bleachers, the pyramid grew quickly.

Suddenly, there was Lucy, standing at the very top. She threw her arms high into the air and smiled down at everyone in the crowd.

The Camdens went wild! Jumping to their feet, they exploded into applause. Tia and the other people in the bleachers joined in. The competition was now over.

Fifteen tense minutes later, the scores were finished being tallied. The head of the cheerleading squad stood up to announce the name of the newest cheerleader at Walter Reed Junior High—Lucy Camden!

Rev. Camden was so proud of his daughter that he took his family out to a late lunch. Tia was invited, too. Everyone had a wonderful time, most of all Lucy.

As the meal ended, Tia watched the Camdens. She saw how they were so comfortable with one another and how they talked and shared their feelings. And she saw how they cared about each other, even when they didn't always agree.

Tia wondered if she would ever have a home like the Camdens'. She knew it would be hard to leave their family.

That night, Rev. and Mrs. Camden mysteriously vanished into the living room. Mary and Lucy were told to put Ruthie and Simon to bed. Matt was given strict instructions not to go anywhere. He and Tia were to remain in the kitchen. They both sat at the kitchen table. The house was quiet and they were alone.

"This was a great day to be with your family," Tia said. "I want to thank you for including me."

Matt took her hand, and Tia looked up at him.

"Listen, Tia," Matt said. "I have to talk to you."

She nodded. "Sure, Matt," she replied.

"I kind of get the feeling that you're not here with me because of *me*," Matt said. "I think you're with me because of my family."

Tia looked into his eyes. They both knew this was the moment of truth. Then Tia looked away, and Matt knew her answer.

"I'm…I'm sorry, Matt," she whispered. "I like you, I really do. But I guess I need more than a boyfriend right now." As she spoke, she squeezed his hand.

"That's okay," Matt said finally. "I understand."

"Please don't take it personally," said Tia.

Matt smiled weakly. "Don't worry," he replied. "I won't. I've been dumped before."

Tia shook her head in disbelief. "You're kidding."

"Nope," Matt said with a shake of his head. "But I was never dumped by anyone I cared about this much."

Then he smiled. "But, hey, sometimes these things don't work out."

Tia nodded. "I know about that."

Matt reached out and took Tia into his arms. As he squeezed her one last time, he fought back the pain. "I'll be fine," he whispered into her ear. "You'll see."

Tia broke the embrace. "Could I ask a terrible question?" she said.

"You bet," Matt replied.

"When things finally settle down and I get my life together, could we try going out again?" She looked hopefully into his eyes.

"That's not a terrible question," Matt replied. "Sure we can." Then he kissed Tia.

For one last time.

NINE

While Matt and Tia talked in the kitchen, Rev. and Mrs. Camden ushered their first guest into the living room. They offered Mrs. Jackson a glass of iced tea and directed her to the couch.

Tia's mother turned to Mrs. Camden. She spoke quickly and seemed uncertain of what to expect. "When you called and said you had someone you wanted me to meet tonight, I hung up the phone, ran to the nearest department store, and blew almost half of my commission on this new dress." She babbled nervously, her words tripping over each other.

"So how do I look?" she asked.

"Lovely," Mrs. Camden nodded.

"So," Mrs. Jackson said to Rev.

Camden. "Is this person I'm supposed to meet an associate of yours, Reverend?"

The Camdens both smiled nervously. "It's Eric," the reverend insisted. "Please, call me Eric." Then he sat down opposite Tia's mother.

"And no," he replied. "The person I want you to meet is not an associate. He's just a...friend."

"Not that I don't go out on dates," Mrs. Jackson added. "I do go out, but it's just so nice to meet new men."

Just then, the doorbell rang. Rev. Camden jumped up to answer it as Mrs. Jackson talked on.

"It's so hard to meet anyone decent at my age," she continued. "Especially when you have a kid attached and everyone in town knows your big-shot husband."

Mrs. Camden winced at her words. At that moment, Rev. Camden returned with Mr. Jackson.

Mrs. Jackson jumped to her feet in shock. "What's this?" she cried. "Some kind of joke?"

Mr. Jackson reacted, too. "I thought you said you had someone you wanted me to meet," he said angrily.

Mrs. Camden looked at the man square

in the eyes. "We do," she replied. Rev. Camden slid the double doors open, and Tia stepped into the room. Her arms were folded protectively. She met her parents' baffled stares head-on.

"Ellen, Bob," Rev. Camden announced. "I'd like you to meet your daughter, Tia…"

Mr. and Mrs. Jackson traded astonished looks. Both of their faces were flushed with embarrassment. Rev. Camden was relieved to see that Tia's parents both realized what they had been doing.

Mrs. Camden rose and put her arm around Tia, who moved into the room and sat down. She faced her parents.

"Apparently, you've both been pretty wrapped up lately," Rev. Camden said. "Wrapped up with your own lives, with your work, and with the pain of your divorce."

He paused and looked at the Jacksons. Neither of them could make eye contact with him.

"Which is too bad," he continued. "Because you're missing out on getting to know a terrific young woman."

Tia smiled at Rev. Camden. He smiled back and stepped to the door. "Your daughter has a few things she'd like to say to you," Rev. Camden said as he looked at Tia.

Tia looked at her dumbstruck parents. Then she cleared her throat and was about to speak when Mrs. Jackson interrupted.

"If there's a problem, dear, you know you can always talk to me."

Mr. Jackson shot his ex-wife an angry look. "Oh, like she can't talk to me?" he barked.

"Why don't we all just *calm* down," Rev. Camden urged. He turned to face Tia.

"Go ahead, Tia."

Tia turned to face her parents. "Ever since the divorce, I feel like neither of you really care about me."

Both parents opened their mouths to object, but the reverend silenced them.

"All you care about is getting back at each other," Tia accused them. "Nobody listens to me. Nobody ever asks me what I want. All you ever ask me is what the other one is doing. And I'm tired of it. I'm tired of being shuffled back and forth."

Tia looked at her father. "I'm tired of sitting in your house alone, Dad." When Mrs. Jackson smiled at that, Tia turned on her.

"Or in your condo alone, Mom. I need

you to be there. I need you both to be there. Even if I have to settle for you guys one at a time…"

Mr. Jackson cleared his throat. He spoke softly. "Why didn't you say something sooner, sweetheart?" he asked.

"When, Dad?" she replied, her dark eyes flashing. "When you come home for five minutes while you change for your next date?"

Mrs. Jackson smiled again. And again, Tia turned on her.

"And you don't talk to me either, Mom," she cried. "If you did, you'd know that I don't want to move into some stupid singles condo."

Mr. and Mrs. Jackson exchanged guilty glances. Tia rose from her chair. She was standing tall.

"So that's all I wanted to say. For now, anyway. And I hope I didn't hurt your feelings too much, because I love you both…"

Tia paused.

"Even if you don't love each other anymore." Then she moved to the door.

"I'm going to ask Matt to drive me home," she said over her shoulder. Mrs. Camden closed the door behind them, and

Rev. Camden was alone with Mr. and Mrs. Jackson.

On the other side of the sliding doors, Tia leaned against Mrs. Camden.

"That was the hardest thing I've ever done," she whispered.

"I know," Mrs. Camden replied. "But you had to do it. And you did great."

"Do you think they're gonna hate me?" Tia asked fearfully.

"Oh, no, no," Mrs. Camden insisted, holding the girl close. "You have to believe that this is all going to work out for the best."

Tia looked up into Mrs. Camden's eyes. "I think that all of you Camdens believe in miracles," she said.

"It comes with the territory," said Mrs. Camden.

"Do you know what, Mrs. Camden?" Tia said, smiling weakly. "I think I'm beginning to believe in miracles, too."

Mrs. Camden hugged Tia. A moment later, Matt came around the corner. He cleared his throat.

"Here's Matt," Mrs. Camden said. "He'll take you home."

Tia nodded.

"Good-bye, Mrs. Camden," Tia said. "And thank you. Thank you for everything..."

"Look," Rev. Camden said, facing Mr. and Mrs. Jackson. "I'm sure you know your daughter best, but I've talked to a lot of kids whose parents are going through a divorce. It's very easy for them to feel that no one cares about them. Some kids in Tia's situation can handle it. They understand that their parents still love and care about them. But others don't do so well. Some run away. Some even do...more drastic things."

The reverend paused, giving his words time to sink in.

"These children become the victims of the people who aren't paying attention to them because they're in pain themselves."

Again, Mr. and Mrs. Jackson's eyes met. But this time, they didn't turn away from each other. "I think we're getting your point," Mrs. Jackson said.

"I'm sorry," Rev. Camden said. "I don't mean to push. I just want to do what's best for a terrific young woman. And I'm sure that the two of you feel the same."

Then Rev. Camden rose and left the

room. He slid the door closed behind him, leaving the Jacksons alone to work out their differences.

Mr. Jackson rose and stared at the door. "Is it me, or does that guy have a holier-than-thou attitude?" His normal, aggressive tone of voice had returned.

"Boy, does he," Mrs. Jackson said, nodding. "I just hate to think that he's right."

"Yeah," Mr. Jackson muttered. "Me, too."

Mrs. Jackson gave an ironic smile. "Look at that," she said. "We just agreed on two things."

To their surprise, they both laughed nervously. Then Mr. Jackson spoke. "Do you think Tia would like it if we made an appointment with the reverend and the three of us sat down to talk?"

Mrs. Jackson's smile brightened.

"Three in a row," she announced.

Then Mr. Jackson extended his hand and helped his ex-wife to her feet.

"Let's go visit with *our* daughter," he said. Mrs. Jackson nodded.

"Bob," she replied. "I couldn't agree with you more."

TEN

The next evening was less eventful for the Camdens. Matt was at the library doing research for his paper. Mary and Lucy were hanging out in their room. Ruthie had gone to bed early and was sleeping soundly.

The only interruption was a phone call. Mrs. Camden looked up from her book as her husband answered it. He carried the phone into the study and talked for a long time.

Mrs. Camden heard her husband rummaging in the closet after the phone conversation was over. Curious, she went over to him.

"Who was on the phone?" she asked.

Rev. Camden stuck his head out of the closet. "Oh, that was Bob Jackson," he replied.

"Oh?" she said, surprised.

"Yeah," Rev. Camden continued. "It seems he and Ellen are looking for a qualified therapist to help Tia through this difficult time. They wanted me to suggest someone, so I gave them a few names and numbers."

"That's good," Mrs. Camden said.

"At least it means they're talking," he replied. "That's got to count for something. And they're all attending the counseling sessions together—like a family."

"Wow!" Mrs. Camden said, clearly impressed. "I guess you can do just about anything you put your mind to."

"I call them as I see them," he joked.

Just then, he pulled a cloth-wrapped package out of the closet. His wife looked at him curiously. When he dove back inside the cramped space, Mrs. Camden interrupted him.

"Now that you've fixed everyone else's problems, do you think you might have a few minutes for me?" she said.

"Sure," said the reverend. Then he

came out of the closet and closed the door. He handed his wife her coat.

"What's going on?" she said, puzzled.

"Well, it's…never mind, honey. It'll be easier if I just showed you."

Lifting the cloth-draped bundle in his arms, Rev. Camden turned to his wife.

"Follow me."

As they went up the stairs together, they passed Simon on the landing. His eyes were closed and he was chanting his invisibility mantra over and over in his head.

"Say, honey," Rev. Camden remarked. "Do you have any idea where Simon is?"

"No," Mrs. Camden replied innocently. "I haven't seen him in a long time."

As they continued up the stairs, Simon opened his eyes and mouthed a silent "Yes!"

At the top of the steps, husband and wife chuckled together.

"Now what is this all about?" Mrs. Camden demanded.

"You'll see," answered the reverend.

In her bedroom, Lucy was admiring herself in the mirror. *This cheerleader sweater looks pretty good,* she thought to herself.

Mary came up behind her.

"Do you want to see the locomotive cheer again?" Lucy asked excitedly.

"No, no," Mary insisted. "That's all right."

"Do I look good in my sweater?" Lucy asked.

"You look great," Mary admitted. "And I have to say that you looked great yesterday afternoon, too."

"Thanks, Mary," Lucy said.

"Oh!" Mary cried. "I almost forgot." She raced over to her dresser and opened the top drawer. She took out a gift bag and handed it to her younger sister.

"I got you a little present," she said.

Lucy smiled and took the bag. Then she peeked inside.

"Oh, wow!" she exclaimed. "A sports bra!"

"Yep," Mary nodded. "I thought since you're kind of an athlete now, you might need it."

Lucy smiled and hugged her sister. "Thanks, Mary," she cried. "You're the best."

"One other thing," Mary said.

"Yeah?"

"Who taught you how to stretch?"

"Matt," Lucy answered.

"That's what I thought."

"Why? Did I do them wrong?" Lucy asked anxiously. Mary shook her head.

"You didn't do them wrong, but there are different kinds of stretches for different kinds of exercise." She took Lucy by the hand. "Here," she said, "let me show you…"

Rev. Camden took his wife's hand and led her out onto the roof of their home. The night was clear and balmy. The stars shone brightly.

He set down his bundle and pulled the cloth away. Mrs. Camden saw a picnic basket and the reverend's old guitar. She smiled and hugged him.

As she sat down, Rev. Camden popped a bottle of expensive champagne. He poured two glasses while she rummaged through the basket.

"Expensive champagne and caviar?" she remarked. "How did you afford this?"

Rev. Camden sat down next to her, cradling his old guitar. He strummed a few chords.

"I was saving up for a new guitar," he said. "But I decided I could get by with a few new strings instead."

As she listened, sipping the champagne, Rev. Camden began to play.

It was a song Mrs. Camden used to love to hear her husband play when they were young, an old tune called "Up on the Roof."

"We came up here the night we moved into this house," Rev. Camden said. His wife smiled at the memory.

"I remember," she sighed.

"Oh, yes." He fumbled inside his coat pocket. "I wanted to give you this, too."

"What is it?" she asked, holding the paper in her hand.

"Just a little poem I wrote this morning," he replied. "Instead of this week's sermon."

Mrs. Camden beamed. "Is it for me?" she asked.

"Only for you," he replied. "It's called 'Time Enough and Love Enough.' I dedicated it to you. I hope you like it."

"I know I will," she replied, kissing him tenderly.

Then Mrs. Camden leaned against her husband as he played. Soon they were singing the familiar words of years past.

As the music descended over the house, a cool breeze blew, stirring the leaves on the trees. Somewhere in the peaceful night, an owl hooted. And Rev. and Mrs. Camden sat together on the roof of their home, counting their blessings.

Each and every one of them.

7th Heaven

"THE LITTLE SHOW THAT COULD"

In 1996, a brand-new drama premiered on national television. It was a family-friendly show about traditional values, and it revolved around a nuclear family living in a quaint American town. But this was not just any family.

The show was about the Camdens, a family that consisted of a minister, his wife, and their five (now seven!) children. Exploring the life of a man of God and his family was an unusual concept for television. Appropriately titled *7th Heaven* (as there were then *seven* members of the Camden family), the show came to the attention of the brand-new WB Network.

Because of its late arrival to network television, the WB was not yet available in every city in the United States. Its audience was still small, though growing by leaps and bounds. The WB Network was willing to take a risk on a show that did not fit the usual formula. They wanted something unique.

7th Heaven was that show.

The new series was the brainchild of a talented woman named Brenda Hampton. She based her idea for the show on a simple concept: "What if there *is* a functional family in America?" Her vision was of a happy, loving American family—something not often portrayed on network television. But according to one *TV Guide* article, that was just the hook she needed to get a major producer interested in the show.

"Brenda throws her heart and soul into every show," said Stephen Collins, who plays the head of the Camden household. "She is genuinely inspired by the people she is writing about."

But Brenda Hampton knew she could not create a television show without a producer. So she approached one of the single most successful television producers of all time.

Aaron Spelling was already famous for such high-profile hits as *Love Boat, Beverly*

Hills, 90210, and *Melrose Place.* A giant in the industry, he had produced over one hundred television shows in his long career. Spelling also liked to take risks. And after he met with Brenda Hampton, Spelling fell in love with the *7th Heaven* concept. He decided to take another risk—and *7th Heaven* was born.

SOMETHING DIFFERENT

By putting faith in *7th Heaven,* Mr. Spelling was offering his viewers something different from the type of shows that had made him a television mogul.

7th Heaven was so different, in fact, that the other networks—ABC, CBS, NBC, and FOX—all said no. Only the WB was willing to give the show a chance.

The network ordered a half-season's worth of programs, or thirteen episodes. Although it wasn't a full season of twenty-two episodes, it was a start.

Soon an appealing cast was assembled. Brenda Hampton had said that her goal was "to create a show that families enjoy watching." What she didn't expect was for the cast and crew of *7th Heaven* to bond as if *they* were a family themselves. But that's exactly what happened.

"We have such a great time together that we feel like a family," said Jessica Biel, who plays oldest daughter Mary Camden.

With a happy cast, a hardworking writer, and a television genius for a producer, *7th Heaven* began production.

THE DEBUT

Everyone who saw the first episode of *7th Heaven* in August, 1996, agreed that the show was unlike anything on television at the time.

For one thing, *7th Heaven* wasn't flashy. Instead of the usual glitz and glamour, the show had a kick-off-your-shoes, homespun feel that was comforting, even old-fashioned. It reminded television viewers of shows like *The Waltons* and *Little House on the Prairie*.

But *7th Heaven* wasn't all sugar-and-spice or feel-good fluff. The scripts balanced sentiment with cutting-edge stories that dealt with real issues. And the show had a very attractive cast of young performers who were fresh and vibrant.

What *7th Heaven* didn't have were phenomenal special effects or breathless car chases. It didn't have sensational soap opera plots or mysterious murders. And it didn't star a cast of former runway models wearing glamorous fashions as they posed in expensive, exotic settings.

7th Heaven started as a small show by today's television standards. But it was a small show with a very big heart. It dealt with the kind of dilemmas that most people wrestle with at one time or another.

At its core, *7th Heaven* is the story of an American family led by a devoted minister named Eric Camden and his loving wife, Annie. The series features members of Eric's church congregation, as well as some of the people in the local community. But most of the action on *7th Heaven* revolves around the Camdens' large family, which originally consisted of three teens and two young children. (Down the road, the family was joined by a dog named Happy and twin baby boys.)

With drama—and plenty of humor— *7th Heaven* explores how each member of the Camden family faces life and relates to his or her world and to each other. But most of all, *7th Heaven* is filled with love.

Lots and lots of love.

LONG, HARD ROAD TO SUCCESS

Before *7th Heaven,* the WB Network was probably best known for the weekly adventures of a certain foxy, teenage monster hunter. Unlike *Buffy the Vampire Slayer,* however, *7th Heaven* was not an instant hit. In fact, the show was in trouble at the start.

Maybe *7th Heaven* was just *too* different.

When the first hour-long episode premiered, there weren't many programs on network television that an entire family could enjoy together. The few exceptions, like *Home Improvement* and *The Nanny,* were sitcoms. Though half-hour comedies are entertaining, it's nearly impossible to delve into complex problems in just thirty minutes—and stay funny at the same time.

7th Heaven filled that gap. It was the first television series to appear in a very long time that attempted to explore the joys and pains of family life in both a dramatic *and* a funny way. Before *7th Heaven,* and outside of a few rare sitcoms, audiences usually found family-friendly fare only on cable stations like TVLand and Nick at Nite.

Despite the show's many blessings, however, *7th Heaven* struggled to find an audience in its first season. It debuted at the bottom of the ratings charts. And it pretty much stayed there, week after week.

7th Heaven's future was beginning to look grim. Things got so bad that it seemed as if the show might be canceled before it even had a chance to shine.

Fortunately, the creator, the producer, and the cast all believed in the show. And they soon convinced the folks at the WB to stick with it. But even with the network's support, the show finished its first season with very low ratings.

It seemed as if no one was watching the Little Show That Could.

Finally, during its second season, the

good word about *7th Heaven* began to spread. Slowly and steadily, the show's audience began to grow. Critics and media-watchers began to sit up and take notice, too.

By the end of that second season, things were moving in the right direction. *7th Heaven* finished as the second-highest-rated show on the WB, right behind *Dawson's Creek*.

But because the WB Network was very small, the show's audience—when compared to that of shows on the big, established networks—was small, too. The show was ranked at 103 on the Nielsen ratings chart, which meant that more viewers watched 102 other shows than watched *7th Heaven*.

Then the long-awaited miracle happened. The kids of America discovered *7th Heaven!*

SUCCESS AT LAST

Suddenly, children and teenagers alike began to watch the show—and loved it! They thought it was sweet and wise, funny and clever. But above all, they thought it was *real*. (And they were psyched about the good-looking cast, too.)

Teens in particular found something cool about a show that didn't feature gun-toting bad guys or psycho-killers. Finally, there was a show that seemed to understand what they were going through. And it wasn't long before their fathers and mothers were watching, too.

Adults enjoyed the sympathetic way the Camden parents were portrayed. Television shows often seem to depict parents as silly, incompetent, or both. Not *7th*

Heaven. Brenda Hampton and Aaron Spelling chose to portray real, three-dimensional characters to depict true-to-life parents in Eric and Annie Camden.

7th Heaven found its most loyal and enthusiastic fans in teen and preteen girls. They loved *7th Heaven*'s mix of comedy and crisis. And many of them developed major crushes on two irresistibly cute members of the cast, Barry Watson and David Gallagher.

By the time the third season began, *7th Heaven* had become a full-blown phenomenon. It was declared the fastest-growing drama on television. In fact, the show was becoming so popular that viewers were eager to see the early shows they had missed. That led to the WB's decision to run *7th Heaven: Beginnings*, in addition to the brand-new episodes. Suddenly, the little show that not many people had known about became the little show that won the hearts of America.

In 1999, *7th Heaven* became the weekly show most watched by young adults. The February 8 episode, which featured the birth of the Camden twins, David and Samuel, was the highest-rated hour-long show in the WB Network's history. Then the March 6, 1999, issue of *TV Guide* pronounced *7th Heaven* the "best show you're not watching."

But actually, you *are* watching. Millions of Americans now tune in to the WB Network to watch the show twice each week. They want to laugh and cry with the most loving and popular family in America.

And it's quite a family!

MEET THE CAMDENS

Fans of *7th Heaven* are captivated by the show's wonderful characters, who are portrayed by a cast made up of both established actors and exciting, talented newcomers.

Here's your chance to meet each member of the Camden family, as well as the performers who play them.

Eric Camden is the head of the Camden
family. He is also an inspiration to and spir-
itual leader of his church congregation in
the all-American town of Glenoak.

Eric has dedicated his life to helping
others, which sometimes leads to late-night
calls for his help in crisis intervention.

His own no-nonsense father is a retired
military officer, so Eric moved around a lot
while he was growing up. This may explain
why he insisted on setting down strong
roots in Glenoak and getting involved in the
community.

In college, Eric received the call to
become a minister. His career choice didn't
sit well with his father at first, and that
caused some tension between the two men.

Eric met Annie, his future wife, while

they were both in college. She supported Eric's decision to become a minister. Now even Eric's dad agrees that his son made the right decision. Though they still have some tense moments, things are much better between the two of them.

The Camden kids all love and respect their grandfather and look forward to visits from the man they call "the Colonel," which makes Eric very happy.

As a community leader, Eric Camden's job is to help all kinds of people in difficult situations. For instance, Rev. Camden has talked a young boy out of suicide, helped a troubled drug user kick his deadly habit, and assisted an abused spouse who needed to escape her husband.

Sometimes Eric's professional life and home life clash, and he finds it hard to juggle his parishioners' wishes with the needs of his family. But with faith—and a healthy dose of optimism—Eric Camden finds the strength that he needs to endure.

Eric also has a hidden side. He plays guitar and sings, and was once a member of a rock-and-roll band!

Eric Camden is played by Emmy Award–nominated actor STEPHEN COLLINS, a popular Hollywood actor who divides his time among television, motion pictures, and the theater.

Born in Des Moines, Iowa, and raised in New York, Collins co-starred as Sela Ward's love interest in the dramatic series *Sisters* before winning his role in *7th Heaven*. His handsome good looks and great talents also landed him the role of President John F. Kennedy in the miniseries *A Woman Named Jackie*.

Many fans may remember Collins as Captain Decker in the first Star Trek film, *Star Trek: The Motion Picture*. More recently, he appeared in *The First Wives Club*.

In addition to his busy acting career, Stephen Collins is a bestselling author. He has written two novels, *Double Exposure* and *Eye Contact*. Collins is currently at work on a third book.

As soon as he was cast in *7th Heaven*, Collins threw himself into the role of Rev. Camden. He spoke to ministers all over the country to do research for his part.

Annie is the calm center of the storm that is the Camden household, always providing the nurturing and support her family needs. She is the glue that holds the family together. She is also a whiz at electronics and is in charge of many of the household repairs.

An intelligent and educated woman, Annie chose motherhood over a high-powered career in business. Though some women might not understand her choice, Annie has never looked back or experienced any regrets. In her heart, she knew that she was making the right decision for everyone.

Annie was extremely close to her own

mother and suffered terribly when she passed away. To make matters worse, she felt very uncomfortable when her father remarried a few years later. Both of these traumatic events happened not long before the birth of her twin boys, David and Samuel. Annie will always regret that her mother never had the chance to get to know the newest additions to her family. However, Annie's faith, determination, and love for her husband and children enable her to overcome even the greatest obstacles.

Because she is a minister's wife, Annie is often in the public eye. While some people might enjoy this attention, Annie doesn't like it at all. However, she views being in the spotlight as an unavoidable part of her husband's profession. She is even-tempered and readily accepts her position.

Annie is a strict but loving parent. She has a deep understanding of each of her children and is often very protective of them. She is calm during crises and freely dispenses wise advice.

The character of Annie Camden is played by actress CATHERINE HICKS.

Catherine Hicks was born in Scottsdale, Arizona, and is a graduate of Cornell University. She celebrates her birthday on August 6.

She began her career on daytime television in the critically acclaimed soap opera *Ryan's Hope*. She has also appeared as a regular on several other television series, including in a co-starring role in another Aaron Spelling production, *Winnetka Road*.

In 1981, Hicks was nominated for an Emmy Award for her role as Marilyn Monroe in *Marilyn: The Untold Story*. And, like her *7th Heaven* co-star Stephen Collins, Hicks has a Star Trek connection. She played a pivotal role as a scientist in *Star Trek IV: The Voyage Home*, opposite William Shatner's Captain Kirk.

More recently, Hicks appeared with Lauren Holly and Ray Liotta in the action film *Turbulence*.

> *NAME:* MATTHEW CAMDEN
> *OCCUPATION:* College student and big brother
> *HARDEST JOB:* "Trying to keep Mary and Lucy in line. It's a full-time job!"
> *MOST EMBARRASSING MOMENT:* "I won't give Mary the satisfaction of repeating it, but you *know* she was the cause."

Matt is the oldest kid in the Camden clan, a position that brings a lot of pressure with it. Not only does he have to deal with the trials and tribulations of growing up a minister's son, he also has to be a role model for his younger brothers and sisters.

From a long-haired, somewhat rebellious teenager, Matt has grown into a very responsible young adult. After graduating with honors from the public high school in Glenoak—and flirting with the ideas of moving to California or joining the army—Matt went on to attend the local university.

While Matt is a hero to his younger brother Simon, he is sometimes regarded by sisters Mary and Lucy as a dictator. That's because, where his sisters are concerned, Matt is...well, a bit *protective*.

"I know trouble when I see it, and my

sisters are *trouble*," Matt once said.

Though he has had several casual girl-friends, and a serious relationship with a young deaf woman named Heather, Matt often seems clueless when it comes to members of the opposite sex. And Matt's troubles with women are a constant source of amusement to his oldest sister, Mary. Although he is sometimes forced to take on responsibilities far beyond his years, in most ways, Matt Camden is a typical 18-year-old.

Matt is played by **BARRY WATSON**, who was born in Traverse City, Michigan, on April 23, 1974. Barry was a mischievous kid. But luckily, he had an imaginary friend called Booey to blame for his misbehavior.

"Anything bad I did, I blamed it on Booey, the evil twin I created."

(Fan note: Booey turned up as Ruthie Camden's imaginary friend in a 1999 episode of 7th Heaven.*)*

By the time he was eight years old, Barry's good looks and natural ability in front of a camera had already won him modeling jobs. But Barry didn't want to live the glamorous life of a fashion icon. "I was doing some modeling," Barry explained to *Teen Beat* magazine. "I was young and thought it was really stupid. I just wanted to be a kid, so I quit."

As it turned out, fashion modeling's loss was the theater's gain. Not too long after his modeling career ended, Barry turned to acting. But like many teens just starting out in a high-powered career, Barry did things a little backward.

"I started auditioning and doing theater and regional commercials," Barry remembers. Only then did he start taking acting classes and seminars. Luckily for *7th Heaven* fans, Barry quickly got over his "just being a kid" idea and was bitten by the acting bug. A talent agent came to Dallas and saw Barry perform. "[The agent] pulled me aside and asked me if I wanted to come to Los Angeles. I said, 'Sure!'"

Success came quickly after that. Barry's first California acting job was a part in a toy commercial. Once he was established in Hollywood, Barry soon became a regular on TV commercials.

But Barry's family always stressed the importance of an education. No matter what career path their son ultimately took, they wanted him to finish school. So it was not until after he graduated from high school that Barry's serious acting career really took off.

First came a number of bit parts for the six-foot, 170-pound actor with the long brown hair and hazel eyes. Barry appeared in *Baywatch; The Nanny; Sister, Sister;* and the daytime drama, *Days of Our Lives*.

Television series work soon led to TV movies, with Barry appearing in such films as Daryl Hannah's remake of the classic 1950s science fiction movie *Attack of the 50-Ft. Woman*. He also appeared in a poignant film called *Marina's Story,* about the wife of John F. Kennedy's assassin, Lee Harvey Oswald. After that, Barry took a small part in the feature film *The Circle Game*.

His work—and his obvious charms— soon landed Barry a gig as a recurring character on a television show called *Malibu Shores*. The show was short-lived, but it did give Barry some vital TV series experience.

It also put Barry in touch with two young actresses who would later make their mark on the WB Network—Keri Russell of *Felicity* and Charisma Carpenter of *Buffy the Vampire Slayer*.

Aaron Spelling, who had produced *Malibu Shores*, spotted Barry's phenomenal talent early on. The producer knew he would cast the young heartthrob in a future show.

Then along came *7th Heaven*.

Barry instantly related to both the show and his character. He explained his feelings to a reporter from *16* magazine during the show's first season: "I'm kind of like my character in a sense. He cares a lot about his family. He truly does. I have a really good, close relationship with my siblings, too."

Barry says he is especially close to his grandfather. "He always told me that whatever I do, to just be happy."

It wasn't too long after the debut of *7th Heaven* that the fan mail started pouring in for Barry. And soon, even jaded television executives were impressed by the newcomer's fan base. Some were convinced he was the reason teenage girls were tuning in every week.

"He's such a Rolls," said Tia, a 14-year-old fan from Ohio. "Compared to Barry, Leo [Leonardo DiCaprio] is a tuba."

7th Heaven turned Barry into a star—and a teen obsession—practically overnight. *YM* quickly named him one of the "50 Most Beautiful Guys in the World." Television's *Inside Edition* dubbed Barry one of TV's "Hot Hunks of Fall 1996."

Luckily, Barry took all his fame and fortune in stride and didn't let them change him. Barry is serious about his career, and he's not satisfied with becoming just a sex symbol. He considers himself a professional actor. He cares about his craft and the roles he plays.

In summer 1999, Barry starred in his first major motion picture—*Scream* producer Kevin Williamson's newest thriller, *Teaching Mrs. Tingle*. Barry was able to stretch his acting muscles in a juicy new role, appearing along with Katie Holmes, Molly Ringwald, and Vivica A. Fox. He played one of a group of high school students who kidnap a cruel teacher in a revenge scheme. In July, Barry was also named one of *Entertainment Weekly*'s "100 Most Creative People in Entertainment."

Needless to say, with a successful ongoing TV series like *7th Heaven* and a budding movie career, Barry doesn't have much time to go out on dates. In fact, the 25-year-old hunk doesn't have a steady girlfriend. Instead, Barry spends most of his free time with his family, which includes three younger brothers and sisters.

For fun, Barry likes to go camping and hiking. He also enjoys tennis, skiing, rollerblading, scuba diving, swimming, and surfing.

Barry loves animals and has two dogs, Harsky and Stutch. Their names are a clever play on the title of Barry's favorite old television series, *Starsky and Hutch*.

(Fan note: Harsky is a golden retriever-pit bull mix, and Stutch is a beagle.)

Mary, the second oldest of the Camden siblings, is very different from her brother Matt. She can occasionally be stubborn, willful, and even something of a brat. But Mary would probably describe herself as strong, independent, and *very* cool.

There is one thing—besides sports—that Mary is extremely good at. She uses Matt's sense of responsibility toward her as a tool to get under his skin. In this, she succeeds nearly every time.

Of course, Mary loves her older brother. And even though he may not like to admit it, Matt feels the same way toward his sister.

Mary is a junior in high school. Though she is not one of the most popular kids in her class, she's not a dork, either. She's a very good student, but what she's really known for is her athletic skill.

To put it simply, Mary is a total jock. She loves all sports, but excels at basketball. She is one of the star players on her high school girls' basketball team and takes the game very seriously. She was devastated when she had to sit out part of a season because of an injury to her leg. Mary also suffers from "performance anxiety," which caused her to ban her family from watching her play in a very important game.

Much of Mary's stubbornness is inherited from her strong-willed mother. Mary would never admit to this, however. She sees her mom as being out to thwart her every wish, like the time she wanted to get a tattoo with her teammates.

"Moms always think they know better," Mary once said, adding, "and I guess maybe they *do*."

Mary has a sometimes frustrating relationship with her younger sister Lucy. This problem is made worse by the fact that Mary and Lucy have to share a bedroom.

Though Mary hasn't dated much—most of the guys in school are afraid of being shown up by her athletic skills—she has had a few crushes. Some of her dating experiences have been disastrous, like the time she sneaked away from home to attend a wild fraternity party with an even wilder classmate.

Luckily for Mary, however, she usually has Matt to bail her out. Not that she would ever appreciate her brother's help, though!

Mary's most serious crush was on a guy named Wilson. He was a little older, and had far more experience in terms of dating. Mary—and her family—were shocked to learn that Wilson had a secret past and was the widowed father of a little baby. This revelation changed their relationship in a big way.

Mary is played by 17-year-old newcomer JESSICA BIEL.

Jessica, or "Jessie" as her friends call her, was born in Ely, Minnesota, on March 3, 1982. She spent much of her childhood moving from place to place. While growing up, Jessie lived in Texas, Florida, Connecticut, and Colorado. But moving to all four corners of the United States didn't have a negative impact on Jessie's bubbly personality. In fact, if anything, all that moving around made her even more outgoing and friendly. Wherever Jessie arrived, she quickly made friends.

Like her character, one of Jessie's first loves is sports. "Mary's very athletic," Jessie told *16* magazine, "and I love to play sports, too."

Her favorite games?

Jessie told *Tiger Beat* that she "loves to play football, basketball, and hockey. And I play soccer and [do] gymnastics and swimming and every other sport there is." Lately, Jessie has taken up in-line skating. Watch out, x-treme skaters!

Of course, like her character, Jessie is more than just a jock. She is determined to attend college when she finishes high school, even if it means putting acting on hold for a while.

7th Heaven marked Jessica's television debut. But she was not entirely new to the public eye when she was cast as Mary Camden. Jessie had already done two years of commercial work and fashion modeling.

Even earlier, when she was only eight years old, Jessie began voice and singing lessons. Her music training led to Jessie's passion for acting.

When she moved to Colorado, Jessie began auditioning for regional theater productions. She landed roles in several musicals, including *The Sound of Music, Beauty and the Beast,* and *Anything Goes.* She also found work in local commercials and continued with her modeling jobs.

The skills she developed on stage gave Jessie an opportunity that few young hopefuls get—the chance to be seen by show-business talent scouts.

In Colorado, a talent agency told Jessie to head to California for an annual competition held by the International Modeling and Talent Association.

"So I went to California," Jessie told a reporter. Though her expectations were not high, she was discovered by a famous and respected acting instructor.

"The teacher's name was Diane Hardin," Jessie recalls. "She gave out a scholarship every year to her acting school." Jessie won the scholarship. "I decided to come out and use that so I wouldn't have to pay for acting classes." she said. And best of all, Jessie's parents were behind her one hundred percent!

In 1994, the family relocated to Southern California so that she could pursue her acting dreams. Her stunning figure, green eyes, statuesque build (Jessie is five feet seven inches tall), and boundless energy landed Jessie more modeling gigs.

But it was in 1996 that Jessica Biel

really "arrived": she won the role of Mary Camden on *7th Heaven!* Both Brenda Hampton and Aaron Spelling thought that Jessie was perfect for the role. As Jessie tells it, Mary Camden and Jessica Biel are so much alike that "it's kind of hard to think of something that's different about us."

Since her debut on *7th Heaven*, Jessie has won other parts. She appeared in a film called *It's a Digital World*. Then she played opposite teen heartthrob Jonathan Taylor Thomas in the movie *I'll Be Home for Christmas*. But Jessie got the most attention playing Oscar-nominated actor Peter Fonda's rebellious granddaughter in the critically acclaimed film *Ulee's Gold*.

Despite her busy schedule, Jessie still finds time to model. She has appeared on the covers of *Sassy, YM,* and *Seventeen*. During those rare moments when she's not working, she likes to spend time with her family, especially her little brother, Justin.

Jessie loves her younger brother so much that she invented a very special game for him on his birthday. She hid a thousand dollars from her first paycheck for Justin to find as a treasure hunt. She wanted him to be able to buy the stereo system he'd been dreaming about!

When she's not working or at home with her family, Jessie likes to hang out and act like an average teenager with her best friend, Jesse.

Yes, Jessie and Jesse have almost the same name—and they're real pals!

"I've never had a friend like Jesse," Jessie told *YM*. "She is someone I can be crazy with and also someone I can tell everything to. We can be as wild or as dorky as we want, but our opinion of each other never changes."

What does Jessie think of show business?

She told *TV Guide* that it was harder to get a driver's license than it was to land her part on *7th Heaven*.

"I had no time to do driver's ed," Jessie explained. When she finally landed her permit, she practiced driving on the studio parking lot. Things were going well—until she crashed the family car into a trailer!

NAME: LUCY CAMDEN

OCCUPATION: High school student and
cheerleader

HARDEST JOB: "Going out for the cheerleading squad. The audition was awful,
and my whole family was there to see
it if I messed up. Luckily, things
worked out all right!"

MOST EMBARRASSING MOMENT:
"Every moment I spend living in the
same room with my older sister."

Lucy Camden is the middle child of the
Camden family, which causes her all kinds
of problems. Never mind the fact that she
has to live in the shadow of her older, more
athletic, and (as Lucy sees it) more popular
sister! In many ways, Lucy and Mary are
total opposites. And when it comes to siblings, opposites definitely *do not* attract!

Mary is a member of the basketball
team. Lucy is on the cheerleading squad.
Mary is something of a loner and has few
friends. Lucy is outgoing and personable
and has lots of pals to hang with. Mary
hasn't been much interested in dating.
She's more content with being a good
friend to Wilson. Even though Lucy is
younger than Mary, she has already had a

pretty intense relationship with a boy.

Lucy is much more "boy crazy" than Mary. While Mary refuses to be anything but herself, even to impress guys, Lucy will do whatever's necessary to enter the dating scene. Of course, her parents are there to keep her social life in check!

But these two sisters can agree on at least a couple of issues. For one, they both like to drive Matt crazy. (Lucy actually idolizes her older brother, though she would never admit to it). Also, both Mary and Lucy are able to set aside their differences and conspire to get something they want, like access to the family car, a trip to the mall, or a double date.

After some typical early adolescent awkwardness, Lucy has blossomed into a graceful cheerleader. Gifted with a beautiful singing voice, she is a member of the church choir. Her love life has been put on hold since the birth of the twins. Although she's not happy about that fact, she would never shirk her family responsibilities. At heart, Lucy is a loving, sensitive, and good-hearted girl who is greatly looking forward to growing up.

Lucy is played by **BEVERLEY MITCHELL**,

a talented actress with a big secret. Beverley, who plays Mary's *younger* sister, is really a year *older* than Jessica Biel! Her birthday is January 22, 1981.

Is it hard for the 18-year-old actress to play someone so much younger than herself?

According to Beverley, it is harder to play a member of a big family than it was to play someone younger.

"I've always been an only child, and now I have lots of brothers and sisters," the actress explained. "I cannot picture so many kids and just one bathroom."

As a 15-year-old honor student— and real-life cheerleader—from Southern California, Beverley already had an impressive list of film and television projects under her belt before she joined the cast of *7th Heaven*. She also had a very unusual start in show business.

One day when she was four, Beverley was throwing a tantrum at the mall. A talent agent approached her and asked if she wanted to be an actress when she grew up. Beverley thought about it for a minute— and decided she didn't want to wait!

Her road from typical California kid to Hollywood star was a very short one. Her

Her first professional gig was an AT&T commercial, and many other commercials followed, including two for the Walt Disney videos *Sleeping Beauty* and *Lady and the Tramp*. But what proved to be the pivotal role for Beverley came in a memorable Oscar Mayer commercial. She played a girl who complained that her bun was too long for her hot dog.

From there, Beverley went on to play a seven-year-old on the popular daytime drama *Days of Our Lives*. (That time, she was playing her real age!)

After that, television roles came thick and fast. Beverley appeared in *Quantum Leap, Baywatch, Melrose Place, Big Brother Jake, Phenom,* and *The Faculty*. She also co-starred in several made-for-television movies, including *White Dwarf* and the mini-series *Sinatra*.

Later, Beverley starred in a trilogy of television movies, *Mother of the Bride, Baby of the Bride,* and *Children of the Bride*.

Before long, Beverley had made the jump to the big screen, where she played in two theatrical films—*The Crow: City of Angels* and *Killing Obsession*.

Except for the size of her real family, Beverley thinks she has much in common with the character she plays in *7th Heaven*.

Like Beverley herself, Lucy Camden is "sensitive, she doesn't want people to be mad at her, and she really cares about others."

Beverley showed some of that caring when the pilot episode of *7th Heaven* was completed. To celebrate the event, she bought gifts for everyone in the cast and on the production crew.

"I like to go shopping," Beverley told *16* magazine.

Beverley is also a talented artist. She's into crafts and has made a number of gifts for her friends and fellow cast members.

In her spare time, Beverley likes to go horseback riding or in-line skating (look out, Jessica Biel!). She also enjoys soccer, basketball, swimming, and playing with her cats, Tigger and Casper.

Beverley's beautiful singing voice comes in handy when she plays Lucy. In recent episodes, Lucy has been called upon to sing the newborn twins to sleep, making for some of the most tender moments in *7th Heaven*.

Beverley's role model is actress Jodie Foster. She also likes to watch Winona Ryder and admits to having a crush on actor Sean Connery. "I think he's so masculine," she has said.

One of her most exciting moments came in 1998, when she won a Young Artist Award—Leading Young Actress—for Best Performance in a TV Drama or Comedy Series.

One of the most traumatic events in Beverley's young life—the death of a close friend in a traffic accident—was transformed into a powerful episode of *7th Heaven*.

NAME: SIMON CAMDEN

OCCUPATION: Student and budding entrepreneur

HARDEST JOB: "Delivering the Glenoak newspaper. But it's just a first step toward future economic security and independence!"

MOST EMBARRASSING MOMENT: "The time I baby-sat for Ruthie. She tricked me into letting her tie me up."

Simon Camden is a chip off the old block— his brother! Like Matt, Simon has a strong sense of responsibility. He is practically a second father to his youngest sister, Ruthie, and is best friend to the family dog, Happy.

Of all the Camden kids, Simon is probably the sweetest and the least complicated. Unlike the rest of his siblings, Simon always knows what he wants—and how to get it!

He bugged his parents until he got a dog. He bugged his sister Ruthie until she learned to behave. But even though he can sometimes seem a little single-minded, Simon is also the first member of the Camden family to rush to someone else's aid.

Because Simon is so clever at earning money, he always has a stash of cash. It is to "Moneybags" Simon that Mary, Lucy, and even Matt run if they need a loan. Usually, Simon is generous enough not to charge them interest.

Simon's endless determination sometimes backfires. For instance, when he decided he wanted a girlfriend, he made a list of requirements and set out to find a female who fit his wish list. Fortunately, Simon learned that he didn't always have to be so methodical about *everything*—he found a girl who didn't quite make the grade, but whom he really liked anyway.

Now *that's* maturity.

And make no mistake: Simon Camden is mature beyond his years!

Simon is played by the multi-talented DAVID GALLAGHER, who is also quite a bit like the character he portrays. David knows what he wants and works to get it.

David has two brothers and two sisters—Kyle, Killian, Michelle, and Kelly.

And like Simon, David's best friends are his siblings. The only difference is that, in real life, David is the oldest in his family.

David has a dog, too—a lovable rottweiler named Nomad.

David's hobbies include reading—he was a big fan of the *Goosebumps* books—collecting toys, playing video games, or watching his favorite television show, the medical drama *ER*. His favorite group is Metallica.

Before *7th Heaven*, David appeared in a number of television commercials for Disney, Burger King, and Tyson Foods. Later, he co-starred in several made-for-television movies, including *It Was Him or Us, Father's Day, Bermuda Triangle, Summer of Fear*, and *Angels in the Endzone*.

Like other members of the *7th Heaven*

cast, David also appeared in a daytime drama—the now-canceled show *Loving*.

He even got to play opposite megastar John Travolta in two films, playing John Travolta and Kirstie Alley's son in *Look Who's Talking Now*, and Kyra Sedgwick's son in *Phenomenon*.

Like many other young actors in Hollywood, David Gallagher would like to direct someday. He wants to study film editing and directing when he goes to college. But for now, David is content to be an actor. "This is my life, this job," he says.

David Gallagher was born and raised in College Point, New York. The blond, green-eyed, 14-year-old actor celebrates his birthday on February 9.

NAME: RUTHIE CAMDEN
OCCUPATION: Little kid!
HARDEST JOB: "Keeping all my dolls from fighting with each other."
MOST EMBARRASSING MOMENT:
    "Let's just *not* go there."

Ruthie Camden was once the baby of the family. Things changed with the birth of twins David and Samuel. For all of her childish charm—Ruthie likes to be the center of attention. That was the position she occupied until her little brothers came along. Ruthie is learning to live with the new situation, but she finds it very hard.

Fortunately for Ruthie, she has Simon to help her. The two of them are very close. Ruthie looks up to her brother, and listens to what he tells her—even if she doesn't always obey!

Ruthie is played by talented newcomer MACKENZIE ROSMAN, or Mack, as she is called by her friends and real family.

Before joining the cast of *7th Heaven*, Mack appeared in a Tuffs Diapers commercial.

She was born on December 28, 1989, and she was raised in Los Angeles. She has a little brother named Chandler, who will soon follow in Mack's footsteps—he's just appeared in his first commercial.

In her free time, Mack likes to dance, swim, and skate.

```
+------------------------------------------+
| NAME:  HAPPY THE DOG                     |
| OCCUPATION:  Family pet and Simon's      |
|     best friend                          |
+------------------------------------------+
```

Annie Camden relented to Simon's constant urging and brought a dog home from the pound. Simon named his dog Happy.

Everyone thought Simon would settle down now that he had a pet of his own. There were still a few surprises in store for the family, however.

Happy the dog became Happy the mother when she unexpectedly had a litter of adorable puppies. And poor Happy narrowly avoided death when she ran away from the Camden home.

The Camdens also discovered that Happy had lived with another family before them. Though Happy's previous owners wanted her back, they changed their minds when they saw how much the dog was loved by all the members of the Camden family—especially Simon.

Happy the dog is played by HAPPY, a thirty-pound mixed terrier, who was rescued in real life from a California dog pound by animal trainer Shawn Webber.

After some higher education at Boone's Animals for Hollywood, Happy auditioned for the role of the Camdens' lovable pet—and quickly beat out the competition.

7th Heaven is Happy's first Hollywood role.

And let's not forget the newest additions to the Camden family!

They're newborn twins, bouncing baby boys named David and Samuel.

Interestingly, the "twins" are played by real-life quadruplets (that's *four* babies!) LORENZO, ZACHARY, MYRINDA, and NIKOLAS BRINO.

The quads are the children of Tony and Shawna Brino, a couple from Los Angeles. Lorenzo, Zachary, Myrinda, and Nikolas were born in September 1998 and made their television debut on *7th Heaven* just four months later—two Brinos at a time!

Look for more exciting developments as the Camden twins get a little older—and a little more active, too!

In a recent *TV Guide* article, writer Janet Weeks described a special on-set moment that occurred during the filming of the episode that featured the birth of the twins.

It happened after many days of hard work for the cast. The family was gathered around Annie's hospital bed following the arrival of the newest Camdens. As Annie held David and Samuel, the family sang the theme from the *Mary Tyler Moore* show. As the voices sang "You're Gonna Make It After All" softly, so as not to awaken the babies, director Burt Brinckerhoff whispered to his assistant, "I don't want to say 'Cut' because this is so good."

And so it was. But as beautiful as that

scene was, it was just another heartwarming moment for the audience—and the cast—of this wonderful series.

And you can be sure there will be many more such moments in *7th Heaven*'s future...